refuge

refuge

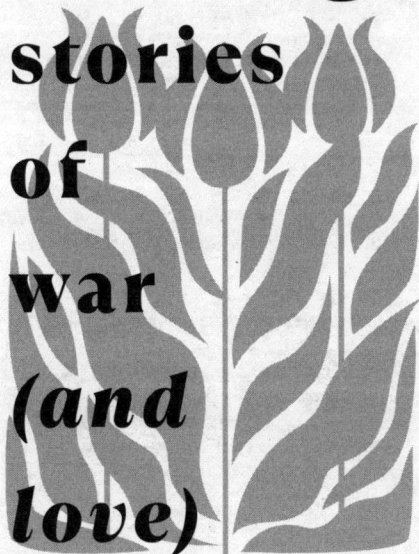

stories
of
war
(and
love)

sunny singh

FOOTNOTE

First published in the UK in 2025 by
Footnote Press
www.footnotepress.com

An imprint of Bonnier Books UK
5th Floor, HYLO, 105 Bunhill Row,
London, EC1Y 8LZ

A CIP catalogue record for this book is
available from the British Library.

ISBN (paperback): 978-1-80444-230-2
Also available as an ebook

1 3 5 7 9 10 8 6 4 2

Typeset by IDSUK (Data Connection) Ltd
Printed and bound in Great Britain by Clays Ltd, Elcograf S.p.A.

MIX
Paper | Supporting
responsible forestry
FSC
www.fsc.org
FSC® C018072

The authorised representative in the EEA is Bonnier Books
UK (Ireland) Limited.
Registered office address: Floor 3, Block 3, Miesian Plaza,
Dublin 2, D02 Y754, Ireland
compliance@bonnierbooks.ie
www.bonnierbooks.co.uk

For Rashmi,
sister by blood, soul and research

Contents

Author's Note   ix

THE TANGO BAR   1
REFUGE   11
KNITTING NEEDLES AND TEA   22
DIPLOMATIC IMMUNITY FATIGUE   35
NUMBER-NINE BUNGALOW   45
THE TIGRESS HUNTS   63
THE WAIT   75
FADED SERGE AND YELLOWED LACE   94
IN THE VAUXHALL PLEASURE GARDENS   102
TULIPS   115
NOT MY MOUNTAINS   132
FRIDAY MORNING COFFEE   150
AMIDST THE DEODARS   165

Previous Places of Publication   183
Acknowledgements   185
About the Author   191

Author's Note

Twenty-five years have passed since I drew up my initial plan for this collection. I wanted to write back to the genre of the Western war story, to examine the ways colonial aspects are minimised and erased there. My planned list of stories spoke back to works by W. Somerset Maugham, Virginia Woolf, Ford Madox Ford and others. At the same time, they drew on Indian writers I loved including Chandradhar Sharma Guleri, Yashpal and Mahasweta Devi. Now completed, the collection draws on beloved writers from across the world.

Soon after creating my plan, I realised that I did not have the necessary knowledge or literary skill to write my stories. More importantly, I understood that I did not have the emotional and psychological maturity to do justice to my characters and storylines. I began working on unlearning what I "knew" about armed conflict and learning from those of us who are forced to experience it.

As my understanding grew, I slowly tackled each story idea. I waited till I had researched further or had the psychological capacity to write it with integrity. I learned about and put in place mechanisms for mitigating the trauma that accompanies any work on violence. As an academic, peer reviews are essential to my writing and I quickly recognised that these must also form part of my creative and ethical practice. I sought out experts, including researchers, activists, artists and survivors, from the culture, place and period of each story. Even when initially upsetting, this expert advice has infinitely enriched and improved each of them.

Finally, and in every case, I only wrote a story when I was certain that my narrative would not cause harm to those who suffered, and continue to suffer, the horrors.

I have learned that writing about violence can be easy if one is willing to dehumanise both the perpetrator and the victim. However, writing about violence while centring the victim-survivor is infinitely more difficult, in part because there are fewer models to follow. It is much harder to write the quiet resilience, courage and strength of victim-survivors than the loud pageantry extended to the victors.

The stories in this collection are set in times of conventional and unconventional wars of the past century.

They confront the unspeakable and unbearable things we humans do to each other. However these are really stories of love, of our infinite capacity for loving our family, friends, neighbours, strangers and ourselves, even in the face of extreme brutality.

Most of all, these stories are a homage to the enduring and comprehensive grace of victims and survivors caught up in wars not of their own making.

The Tango Bar

There is a tango bar in Buenos Aires named El Mirador.
In the wrong part of town. Or at least in the part of town
that Gloria does not usually frequent. And yet tonight,
once again, she sits outside it waiting in the car.

Her hair is pulled up in a tight, conservative bun, a
Burberry trench hides the cheap red dress that she hopes
will help her blend in with the patrons. The fabric clings to
her, itchy and hot, its sheen embarrassing in its discomfort.
She tugs the hem down, then pulls up the neckline, wishing
for an instant for her usual clothes. She feels a flush of
shame and guilt. These should have, ought to have, been
her usual clothes. The car is borrowed too, from one of the
secretaries at work. The seats are vinyl, the engine coughs
at the start, and the pale pink-and-blue plastic Virgencita
hanging off the rear-view mirror makes her cringe.

From the shadowed car, she watches the people stream into El Mirador: women elaborately dressed, their hips swaying unconsciously in anticipation of music; men in worn but immaculately maintained old suits and jaunty fedoras, flirting, laughing, calling out indiscriminate though creatively phrased compliments to the women. The music and the laughter, and the elaborate dance of seduction almost hides the melancholy Gloria knows dwells just beyond the narrowing circle of light that spills out from the bar.

Perhaps tonight, she will gather up the courage to leave her car, to ignore the chafing of the dress against her legs, to walk into that circle of light. Perhaps tonight she will go into El Mirador, not to dance, but to be.

* * *

People forget too easily, Gloria has long thought. Or perhaps it is a deliberate, measured erasure of memory, like her parents wiping away all that came with her birth. Her son has none of her past, not even the shadow of the malevolence that she has long sensed around herself. She has always been proud of her parenting but recently the bright light around her son seems sinister. Her own hair is dark, falling straight and flat against a face that looks nothing like either her Mama's or her Papa's. Not their eyes, not their aquiline noses, not even their narrow jaws. In his infancy, her son seemed to have inherited all of those and she'd told herself that sometimes looks skipped a generation, that she looked like some other ancestor. But as he grows, Alé looks more like her, his jaw widening with each passing birthday, his hair growing coarser, thicker, darker. Sometimes, she catches Papa looking at her child and even through his love, his face grows inscrutable.

Perhaps this is why she has started seeking out the dark places where Papa says she must not go. To the courthouse, and the main library, and more recently to the database held at the Durand, even though hospitals terrify her. She has even been to the website of the old women who gather every Sunday in the Plaza, although she refuses to contact them. And in the past six months, she has come every Saturday night to El Mirador. That is how long she has known.

*   *   *

But Gloria has never wanted to know before. Not for certain, anyway, not the details. Not really. When she decided she had to know, she used her allowance from Papa for the tests. A payback for what he may have taken from her, over the years and so long ago. It hadn't taken her long to get a sample from her mother. Mama drank only single malt and generally too much of it. Gloria helps Mama up the stairs on most nights, guides her into bed and kisses her goodnight. Then she comes back down and tidies up, hiding all the evidence, carefully replacing the whisky in the decanter to the right level from one of the bottles that Mama hides in the cleaning cupboard. Sometimes Gloria thinks Papa knows, but they never speak of it.

That particular night Mama had been crying again when Gloria came home. The decanter was nearly empty and Mama was huddled on the floor, tunelessly humming the same song as always. It is a slow melody, about a woman like the sea.

Mama told her long ago it is about a woman as wild and deep and strong as the sea, with eyes that shine silver like Rio de la Plata in the summer sun. Mama used to hold her hands as she sung it and they would dance slowly around the room, twirling hand in hand across the gleaming floor. Her voice would always hitch just a little on the words about birthing a child for fire, but not for being killed. It is the song that Mama sang to Gloria when she was a child, but always in whispers. She told her it was their special secret, that Papa should never hear her sing or even hum it. Gloria used to think it was a lullaby, but has since learned it is a dirge or perhaps a requiem.

Gloria had sung it with Mama that night as she'd helped her upstairs, her arms wrapped tight around her mother's brittle body. She had gently whispered the words as she kissed her mother's forehead and tucked her under the covers. And she had hummed the song as she wrapped the single tumbler stained with nearly invisible fingerprints and a single red lipstick stain in a snowy-white napkin.

When the results came back, Gloria had wanted to be surprised, heartbroken even. She felt she should grieve. For Mama, the woman who still wouldn't sleep until she knew Gloria was home safe every night. The one who wiped away her earliest tears, who hugged her tight till the pain of a scraped knee was lost in a cloud of love and Chanel No 5, and whose tigress rage terrified away Gloria's suitors, eventually even the father of her son. But Mama wasn't her mother. Not really.

Getting a sample from her father was even easier as Gloria knew, had made sure to learn as a little girl, exactly how Papa liked his things. She could get his socks to line up just right in the top drawer, make sure his shirt collars were always given away when they lost their stiffness. And she alone would make sure his antique silver brush sparkled and shone, and his bone-handled, old-fashioned razor was always sharp enough to draw blood. It had taken her seconds to tuck away a few grey strands left on stiff bristles into an envelope.

Still, she had hesitated before sending off the packet. The best result, she knew, was that Papa and she would not be a familial match. But if the test results proved they weren't – and she prayed for it every night – Gloria promised herself that she'd stop. She'd believe what Mama and Papa had told her long ago. That they had wanted a child. They had wanted her with every bit of their hearts. That her birth parents didn't. They couldn't keep her, another mouth to feed. You know how they are, poor but always having children. So irresponsible. But Mama and Papa loved her, had wanted her, would always cherish her. Protect her.

But Papa hasn't cherished Mama enough. Perhaps he also hadn't cared for that woman who had carried his seed for nine months? She tried not to think of Papa like that – like just another man. Capable of faithlessness. Of deceit. And betrayal. Of inflicting pain.

And with that final thought, even more frightening monsters would rise in her mind. That he had done worse. That she wasn't born of love and light but of terror, agony and horror.

Gloria has known for a long time that Papa has a temper and that sometimes there is blue and purple under the pale makeup that Mama uses. She learned long ago that she must not hug Mama too tight because under the silk and velvet and lace, there are parts of her that hurt when touched. That when Papa asks her for a kiss, she must be careful not to delay because he works so hard and needs to be comforted, and loved by his little girl.

Most of all, she tries not to remember that fight her parents had when she was only twelve.

* * *

Mama never drove past the Plaza. Even on the rare occasions when Jorge drove her in Papa's office car, the big one that made her feel small and a little suffocated behind the dark glass to make sure nobody could see inside, he never drove past that sprawling square. She knew it was there. She read it on the street signs, always in the opposite direction to where she was taken. She had found it on a city map when she was ten, wondering each day why they took the longer ways around.

But on that day, there had been police and army jeeps and big barriers as Mama drove her home from ballet class. Mama had begged the policeman to let her go a different way, even threatened to call her husband. But to no avail. All traffic had been rerouted through the Plaza.

Gloria had been transfixed by the vast rose edifice, a fairy cake that presided over one end. And in front of it was a wide avenue, and a vast stretch, and a garden, and the huge fountain where children played. She stole a glimpse at Mama, whose knuckles shone white on the dark steering wheel. Her jaw was taut, her lips thinned. Her eyes were wide, fixed determinedly on the car ahead.

7

Gloria had felt a sudden twinge of resentment at her parents for withholding this beautiful place from her.

Then she had spotted them. Women who looked a bit like her. With flashing eyes that crinkled but looked straight into the sun, so unlike the languid ones, shielded by dark glasses, of Mama and her friends. With dark hair that hung in plaits or was rolled up in buns, or swished free over their shoulders. They wore clothes that Gloria wanted, meant for comfort and warmth and use. And so unlike Mama's dresses that felt soft against her fingertips when she was allowed to touch them but wrinkled and stained and spoiled almost instantly. She wondered if the women in the square had children they would gather into their arms at any time rather than only when wearing their house clothes.

Papa had been furious when they got home, shouting at Mama so loudly that Gloria hid behind the sofa. When she heard Mama shriek just after the loud clapping sound, she knew she would never ask her parents about the women in the square.

* * *

The tango bar winks and twinkles at her from across the street. The sign above the door is lit up, the curlicued black words – El Mirador – glowing against the yellowed wood. On the top right corner are two smudges, although Gloria knows that up close they turn into portraits.

In her bag are printouts of the same two faces. The woman has feathered hair like Farrah Fawcctt in *Charlie's Angels* and the man has a wide-mouthed smile that she recognises from her mirror. Even though the photographs show only their faces and shoulders, Gloria is sure that they wear bell-bottomed jeans and running shoes with stripes. They look happy in the photos she has in her bag, not resolute and serious like in the painted portraits on the sign. They are young and bright-eyed in both. Isabella and Oscar. Not yet arrested and disappeared.

Inside El Mirador, the lights are dim and dancers twirl and sway and tease, their heads held high, shoulders thrown back. Behind the bar, Raúl serves up the whisky, a cheap local blend that burns Gloria's throat when she gulps it. She doesn't meet his eyes when he wonders why she looks familiar, why he has never seen her before.

But then the music pauses and Gloria sees who she has come to find. The woman she has watched in the Plaza on Sundays, holding her sign, her eyes squinting with fury and determination. Chola. The same woman who dances and claps and sings every Saturday night at the heart of El Mirador. For weeks now Gloria has waited in her borrowed car till the last dancers have left, watching as Chola locks up El Mirador before taking Raúl's arm to slowly walk up the road to their small flat. It is the only time Gloria notices that her shoulders slump, in exhaustion, perhaps even despair.

As Chola nears the edge of the dance floor, with a smile as bright as her red sequinned dress, Gloria notices her hair is greyer than it looks from a distance. Close up, her eyes are strained, their corners deeply lined. But when their eyes meet, the strained look is replaced with something else. Curiosity, apprehension, perhaps even hope.

In her mind, Gloria has practiced this meeting many times. "Soy su nieta," she will say, introducing herself to her grandmother, and Chola will hug her, hold her tight, tell her that she looks so much like Oscar, her son, Gloria's father. That she will stroke her hair and tell Gloria that it is exactly like her mother's. But now, at the edge of the dance floor, words flee both women. They stay like that, in suspended time, for what seems to be a long time, even after another song begins to play and the dancers again wrap their arms around their partners. "Si un hijo quieren de mí . . ."

Abruptly, Gloria breaks her gaze, pushes herself away from the bar, willing herself to run from the milonga, back to where she can breathe, back to Mama. But as she pushes through the dancers, past the woman, Chola grabs her hand to pause her flight, holding her on the swirling dance floor.

When Gloria finally dares to look up, Chola's eyes have lost their strained look. To Gloria, they look like the sea.

Refuge

They fucked the night before she left. With furtive desperation, muffling their giggles against familiar skin, swallowing moans with kisses so as not to awaken Malak in the next room.

Their child barely slept any more, her eyes constantly wide with fear. They looked even more haunted after Nur had cut her curling brown hair short, hoping to pass off her daughter as a boy. That same fear rode Abid, whose hands roamed Nur's skin tonight with something close to panic. And it plummeted down to the bottom of Nur's stomach, leaving desire drowning in terror.

She held on to Abid, her arms wrapped tight around him, trying to memorise every bit of him. The way he called out for her, his deep voice soothing and exciting all at once. "My little bird." His eyes would grow greedy

11

when he said the words in bed. She would blush and drop her eyes when he called her that before their friends, the words both a reminder and a promise. But that night, he didn't call her that even once.

When they talked, it was of practical matters. "Documents must always stay with you. On you. Not in the bag. You remember," his hands pushed away her clothes. She nodded, her mouth pressed to the crook of his neck. "Keep the second phone hidden," his breath grew harsher as his hands kneaded her breasts, massaged the slope of her back. Nur burrowed closer, trying to breathe him all in. "Keep Malak safe. Keep yourself safe." She felt dampness on his cheeks as he pushed into her, slamming again and again, as if to weld them together.

A burst of gunfire sounded on the street just as he came, snapping a yelp from her. She didn't come.

Afterwards, they clung to each other like frightened children, listening to sounds they could not grow accustomed to: the stomp of boots, slammed doors, heavy things being dragged and dropped, the weeping pleas. In the past months, it seemed everyone had lost the ability to scream, to shout. Their despair was as muted as their fear, expressed only in silent tears and gagged pleading.

Holding her as if she were some precious, fragile thing, Abid muttered his list of preparations again, his breath warm against her ear: coats, boots, extra chargers, double cell phones, a wad of mixed currency he had hidden in a volume of Rumi. Nur had cried watching him carefully glue the pages shut, cutting and scraping a little compartment into the block. "My love, you know these by heart." It was the first present she had given him. He would sing her the song of the bird when she cooked their dinner, his rich baritone sending a twinge through her belly.

"Anytime you have wifi, whatsapp me. We will talk." She nodded, not telling him that she was afraid that he would forget her. That his honey-sweetness would find another home, another mouth to love. There were other fears too, much worse ones, but she refused to allow herself to think of those. It was easier to dread his lack of faith than anything worse.

She has her own list: her few bits of jewellery stitched into the lining of her coat, thin wads of money secreted into the thickness of their winter boots, of women's things she will need, grateful that Malak is much too young to require them too.

She has made a pen drive with photographs of all she loves. Her home with shelves of Hafez and Rumi, the bougainvillea glowing fuchsia against her kitchen window, the wisps of lace and silk in her drawers that she got from Damascus to wear for Abid. Only for him. And so many photos of Malak. Her first steps taken in her parents' home on Eid. Her first day at the kindergarten with her hair

13

braided into two thick chestnut ropes. Malak holding on to Abid, laughing as he swung her around like an airplane. She took no pictures of her brother. That would put him in danger if they were found. And her and Malak too, now that he had joined the fighters.

"Come with us," she pleaded again, knowing all his answers already. They were pretending not to flee, had told their neighbours that she was going to see her mother because Malak was not sleeping. Just as they had told them that Malak's hair had to be cut because she had caught lice at school. So many lies were told, by everyone, that sometimes Nur thought there was no more truth. That they had buried everything true with the first barrel bombs.

"I will come soon. I promise." But she could not believe him. Not when bombs fell from the sky. Not when the man from the sweetshop turned shabiha in the darkness of the night. Not when faceless men dragged neighbours away. When Malak's school teacher disappeared. And then the horrors of the shattered bodies that turned up. Or worse the broken people who returned. And through it all, whispers carried names for all the parts of hell on earth – Al Mezzeh. Saydnaya. Tadmor.

Vows made on pillows, with breaths mingling tenderly had no place in such a land.

* * *

At first, she can't believe the message that Abid has come to her. But the boy insists. Abid is here. He is being processed in the big tent. That he is asking for her, and for Malak. She refuses to hope even as she drags Malak through the camp, stomping breathlessly through the mud and chilling puddles to get to the fence that separates the new arrivals.

In the beginning, she had stood at the fence every day, all day, hoping he would come. But the rivers of humans had swirled and swept by without him: innumerable half-familiar, despairing faces. The countless blank eyes that incessantly searched for something. For threats, for loved ones, for hope. Nur had stopped coming to wait at the fence and she still felt an inner revulsion, knowing that her own eyes had grown the same wild look, the one that made her question if they were still human, if she was still herself.

Beside her, Malak whimpers softly, her sobs muffled as always, her hand crushed in Nur's, yet never pulling away.

All at once, he is there. In front of her, just an arm's length from the fence. Thrown up like debris by the waves, like a broken miracle. His mouth opens as if to shout but she can hear nothing. Only when he draws up close, throwing himself at the metal links of the fence, filling her nose with the foul stench of things that cannot be named, she hears her name. "Nur", "Nur", "Nur" – repeated over and over again like a prayer, in a hoarse shattered whisper.

"Your voice?" She pushes her fingers through the fence, feeling his warmth seep into her.

"They took it." He shrugs. Then his mouth is on her fingers, kissing, warming, suckling on their frozen tips like life.

It is only Malak's frenzied whimpers, barely audible against her legs, that bring Nur to her senses. "She's scared of men."

His body flinches as if he's been hit. "No, only from what she has seen." Nur does not know if her words are meant to comfort Abid or herself. "We have a place to live. Tell them that. They don't have to give you quarters. And make sure they add rations on your papers."

He smiles then, warily, a little sadly. "My little bird has grown brave," his warmth lingers on her fingers even after he has turned away to rejoin the stream of crushed men. She wants to tell him that she hasn't grown brave. She has been broken, shattered into survival, for herself and Malak. But he melts into the milling crowd before she can speak.

In the prefab shelter, there is only a single mattress and Nur does not want to string up a blanket and pile up the clothes for Malak to sleep on. Abid is a man but he is also hers. And he is Malak's, even if he frightens her now. When he holds out a hand, Nur notices that his left pinky has been broken in her absence. It has set badly. There is a mark under his ear too, like a bruise that refuses to heal. And at his throat, strange spikes of glossy scars peek out from beneath the collar.

"They came. After you left," he is matter-of-fact.

"Where?"

"Adra."

She has no words, of comfort or of sorrow. So instead, she feeds Malak, covertly watching Abid as he slowly makes his way through food. He is painfully thin, his sweater too large for his now bony frame. His eyes seem overly large too, even larger than Malak's. His jaw, that she so loved, is craggy and sharp and slightly misshapen on one side. His right shoulder is stiff too. On the back of his hand and in the centre of his palms, there are round dark marks.

Burn marks, she knows. She has a similar one on the inside of her right arm. Wound around a cracked bowl, his hands shake, and with the dirt been scrubbed off, she can see that nails have not grown back. She wants to hold him, to touch him, to offer him the only home she can, in her body. In herself. But the months apart become a thousand miles and there is no way to break the silence. Instead they sleep together, huddled under the blankets she has collected over the months. Nur lies still in the middle, her man and her child on either side of her. Malak clings to her arm, shivering with cold or fear until sleep takes her. On her other side, Abid

17

remains stiff as a board, his body emitting heat even though he holds himself apart.

Nur is nearly asleep when his hand reaches out to hers, folding her fingers into his own.

She lets him.

"You kept her safe," even whispers seem to scrape his throat. "My brave bird."

"Not completely."

"But enough." She wants to draw him close, to be held again in his arms. But he stays still, his body stiff and brittle.

It is mid-morning when Nur returns from taking Malak to the camp school. The shelter is so silent that at first, she thinks he has left. That her frail refuge is bereft again. Dim light filters through the shawl she has pinned over the fibreglass window. Abid sits on the mattress, his knees pulled up beneath his chin, his arms wrapped tightly around his legs. His eyes are unseeing but soft, almost inaudible moans intermittently escape his mouth. She watches him in silence for a long time before removing her scarf and putting it aside. She unpins and unravels the single braid that holds her hair, untangling it carefully with her fingers before lowering herself on the mattress next to him.

"24th March, 2013. They guessed she was a girl. I had to do something."

Abid's moans have ceased. He squints until his eyes focus on her face.

"20:50. They finished at 21:35."

His eyes devour her face. Nur reaches out for his hand, the one with the damaged pinky. She raises it to her temple so he can touch a small, unfamiliar scar at her hairline. "One liked rings."

He stares at her for a long moment. Then he nods, slowly moving their linked hands to his face. "12th January, 2013. For questioning. There was an officer. Then two others."

Suddenly she needs to show herself. And to see him. To know precisely what has been shattered, what can be rebuilt, what has been lost forever. He holds her hand still but she uses the other to unbutton her sweater and the shirt below. Clutching his hand still, she pushes up his clothes, baring the chest she thinks she knows so well. But it is a stranger's body that shudders beneath her fingers. Thin, scarred, with signs of pain carved into the beloved skin by brute force. Then in a sudden frenzy, desperate, she pushes his clothes off, not pausing to look further, just wanting to find her way back to him. Pressing herself against him, keeping her mouth, her arm, some part of her touching him, because to lose contact with his skin would be to lose him all over again, she struggles out of her jeans. Finally, naked, shivering, she pushes him back on the mattress, seating herself over him and takes his damaged hand again to guide him over her skin.

"16th May." She led his fingers over a puckered line running from above her left breast to her shoulder. "Turkish. Border guards."

He half-smiles, his eyes glowing softly. "28th January. This one liked to use a blade to slice us up." He guided her hand over his chest where a series of thin scars spread like a deformed fan.

"14th September. Smuggler." She leads his hand to her belly. She had thought she was pregnant after that one.

Her fingers run lightly up his arm and he shudders. "Ticklish, still?" He shakes his head, his breath light on her hair. "February. They did that a lot. All over my back." Her hands are on his shoulder blades, blindly feeling the ripples gouged by a whip.

His hand shifts to her waist, moving to cup her buttocks, then stills as she stiffens. "10th October. I kept Malak safe." She wants to cry but tears will not come.

He lifts her slightly and pulls her down next to him, pulls her head close so he can look into her eyes. Then slowly, carefully, Abid moves her hand over to his crotch. Her eyes widen as she feels the destruction. "14th March. The last time." His whisper is harsher than ever as she searches his face. Something sardonic twists his lips.

"What now, my brave bird?"

She pulls him close, burrowing into his shoulder, breathing deep till she can smell him, truly him, under the fear and the horror and the pain. "Just this," she sighs, pushing herself closer into him than she ever thought possible.

He nods against her skin, drawing her up against himself. Then broken, shattered, unmade, with the light filtering through her old shawl, on blankets full of scents of strangers, they make love.

Knitting Needles and Tea

Knit, purl, knit, purl. Two rows, then reverse. Purl, knit, purl, knit. Marie knows it is nearly too late for her tea. She knows she must rise, stir the embers alive again, set the water to boil. The precious length of muslin lies clean and ready to wrap around the herbs. She never lets her stocks fall too low, trading at the market but more often growing some in the patch beyond the back door, finding others on her walks through the woods. It is a habit she picked up from Tante, picking, gathering, drying each herb in its season, storing them all in tight jars, the safer, more recognisable ones on her kitchen shelves, more dangerous ones in the little hollow space beneath her bedroom floor. Even her skill with the knitting needles was learned from Tante.

"Teach her, please," Maman had wept that day, leading Marie by the hand to the old cottage tucked in the woods beyond village limits. It was not their first visit, as Tante's had long served as a place to hide from the men who came and went from their lives and left little but pain. The cottage was the only place for Maman to heal, and for Marie to grow less afraid. But that was the day Marie had first bled, when Maman had helped prepare rags and moss to place between her legs and warned Marie to stay away from men. She wishes Maman had followed her own advice.

"Women need a way to make money and a way to be free," said the woman who was not family but something more, only ever known to Marie as Tante. "I will show you both." The learning, like the secret hollow, and now the crumbling cottage itself, are the only presents Marie thinks she has ever received.

In the quiet cottage, the faint, regular, metallic rhythm of her knitting soothes her. Her fingers move by themselves as her mind drifts. Memories she tucks away during the day come easily in the night. Of cat-like, amber eyes and dark curly hair pulled into a top knot, of skin the colour of golden oak, the flash of steel wrapped around a muscular forearm that ends in an oddly feminine hand with long, gentle fingers. For an instant, Marie can feel those fingers exploring, caressing, can smell the woodsmoke and sweat and musk that she is sure still lingers on her quilt even after all these weeks.

She can feel the warmth of his mouth on her lips. She had felt admired with him, adored by him. Even perhaps loved, if love could be found where no words were shared.

The embers in the stove have mostly shrunk to ash and her fingers grow numb around the clicking needles and she shivers despite the quilts wrapped around her legs. As frost thickens on the sole small windowpane, she knows her home will only grow colder in the night. Marie folds away her knitting, deciding that the tea can wait until the next day.

*   *   *

Marie has avoided the village since her return last autumn because it is full of soldiers going north to fight. The girls that pass her cottage on market days tell her there are soldiers from everywhere and giggle about men the English have brought from the east, tall dark men with large turbans and big smiles who have come to save them. The soldiers have their own camps but they are making the village rich buying up food and much else. She thinks of the past summer when other soldiers had marched west and filled the city seemingly overnight.

After two years in the city, Marie had learned to avoid the workshop overseer, to keep her head down, to not flinch, to hide the skeins. She had learned, like the other girls who worked there, about the overseer's thick fingers and sour breath. She had remembered to prepare and drink her tea each time. And she had learned to keep her stocks of tea fresh and to quietly pass on small cloth bundles of herbs in exchange for coin, to help the girls who hadn't managed to fully stay out of the overseer's grasp.

But one morning soon after the soldiers arrived, some of them had come to the workshop. That day Marie had learned that a man alone was more tolerable than a dozen. And even a dozen would be more tolerable without the power to command, to force obedience. In the weeks that followed, she had sold more of the tea than ever before, even giving some away. But soon tea wasn't enough and women with bloated bellies sought her skill with her knitting needles. By summer's end, Marie could no longer wash the smell of blood out of her nostrils.

The nights were growing cooler when Marie began her journey south, avoiding soldiers, the enemy and her own, because she has grown sure that men, in peace or at war, only save people, things, for themselves. She stays off the roads and selects only the smallest hamlets for food and information. She chooses trails through forests, woods and fields that veer away from camps and check posts.

Even so, she is caught twice, once by the enemy, then by the French, and let go soon after. After each release, she slows her travel to gather all that will keep her free, seeking parsley, sage, thyme in kitchen gardens at the edge of villages, savin, pouliot mint, artemisia and jacobee in the woods. She begins to wonder if she will need her trusty knitting needle and tries to imagine guiding its tip between her legs all by herself. Tante had made her practice again and again, guide the tip, feel for the part that has a bit of give, stop if the woman complains of pain or begins immediately to bleed. To slowly, carefully move the needle, feeling for obstructions, scraping the womb gently but surely. Marie wishes Tante were still alive to help her as she had helped so many others.

As she nears the cottage in the woods, she feels her underclothes begin to moisten and stops to check for the first spots of blood. The blood is welcome not only because she has grown sick of the taste of thyme and jacobee tea she has prepared for herself each day on the road. She speeds up to reach the only true refuge she has known, to close the door on the world and know that even alone, she is safe in that shadowed, single-roomed home. As the woods on the trail become familiar, she realises that Tante's gift means Marie can save herself, most of the time, and even some others.

* * *

Few came to the little clearing in the woods where a brook forms a pool before flowing further to meet the Marne. Even fewer find it since the war started. Soldiers flowing to the north prefer the ever-increasing bustle of the village when they stop en route to the front. There is money to be made in war and everyone is washing and cleaning, repairing and fetching for the armies. The women who have come for Marie's knitting needle or tea since she returned home are quicker to pay her in cash. For weeks, she has seen no one even at the edges of the woods.

Perhaps that is why Marie freezes in shock when she finds the clearing occupied. Shaded still by the trees, she stares at the half dozen figures that bathe in the pool, their skin the colour of maple and chestnut, oak and mahogany. Long dark tresses float in the waters, wrapping around the bodies like cloaks. For a whimsical moment, she wonders if she has chanced upon some magical wood creatures. But then one turns towards the nearest bank and she nearly screams at the long, dark beard that stretches over the creature's mouth, along the jaw and down the chest.

Marie pulls further back into the shadows as one climbs out of the water, clad in strange loose garments that stick to his wet skin. His long hair covers much of his face and body, trailing down a broad torso and long limbs, all the way down to his knees. It is only a man, Marie realises, unsure whether she is relieved or disappointed. Forgetting to be afraid, she watches him as he gathers his dripping hair with both hands and squeezes excess water onto the grass. Moving to a patch of sunshine, still autumn-warm, he begins to dry the hair with a cloth.

She is mesmerised by the dark hair drying in the sun until some strands gleam an unexpected red-gold. He draws out a comb and begins to run it carefully down the lengths, delicately untangling the knots. There is something curiously feminine about him and the others who join him in the sunshine, tending to themselves with gentle precision. They move like men who know forests and woods, and speak in hushed words that Marie cannot identify. There is a graceful vulnerability in their bodies, their movements ones she has never associated with men.

Her eyes drift to the man she had spotted first. He has moved to the bundle of clothes and is stripping off the loose pale undershirt that still clings damply to his skin. He is young, she thinks, perhaps even younger than her. There is something elegant about the way he grips the cloth as he moves it over his head and down past his hair. She can't imagine how these fey men will survive in the north, how they could be sent to fight at all.

One of them breaks into song, a melody that is strange and melancholy. A strong voice forms strange words that Marie cannot understand, and yet recognises as such acute painful longing that her eyes grow wet. These must be the soldiers from the east that the English have brought, she realises.

Then the young man notices her amidst the trees. For an instant their eyes meet and hold as he stands frozen.

Then he grabs the shirt to his chest, attempting to cover himself. The song ceases as a shout bursts from him.

In the next instant, the men are grabbing their clothes from the ground, turning towards her even as they rush to gather their loose hair, to snatch up their possessions. She takes an unthinking step forward, then hesitates for a moment before realising that the men are mortified.

It is not a reaction that Marie expected. Her eyes flash over them just as the men avert theirs. The embarrassment is now hers as she flushes and then turns to flee through the woods back to her cottage.

* * *

Marie lays out the items carefully on the table before her: the nearly black jumper she has been knitting, a single knitting needle that she has sterilised with boiling water, small jars of every herb Tante has taught her can solve the problem men leave behind with women, and a nearly empty oilcloth pouch. She knows that her decision must come today, that the time to make choices has almost passed. And yet she hesitates, her mind drifting over the past weeks, stuck on the young man she inadvertently embarrassed in the clearing.

* * *

"Vira." He had gestured to himself, falling into step with her the next day. His long hair was concealed by an immaculate dark turban. She should have been wary, but the memory of the men's unexpected modesty and his averted eyes had calmed her nerves. He hadn't seemed to expect an answer, simply walking with her through the woods. As they neared her cottage, she had turned and pointed to herself. "Marie."

He had repeated the name thrice, softly, first as a question, then as if testing the sound on his tongue, and finally stretching it slowly over a broad smile. He hadn't touched her or even tried to enter the cottage, but instead seated himself on the low wall that sheltered her herb garden. And there he had waited, watching her go about cleaning and preparing her harvest for drying, carrying logs from the woodpile into the cottage for the fire, soaking an extra handful of oats for her porridge dinner. She had hoped he would stay to eat with her. Despite the lengthening shadows, his eyes had lingered on her, examining her not as if she was to be possessed or used or torn. Instead he had considered her as if exploring a mystery, or assessing something of great value.

Marie had finished her chores, put the porridge on and then found a spot on the low wall near him. They had watched the shadows lengthen across the garden and then deepen in the woods beyond. She had never imagined that silence could be so comfortable, even companionable.

Vira had drawn an oilcloth pouch from his shirt and opened it to withdraw a packet of something wrapped in plain cheesecloth. He had pulled out a single piece of something the colour of dull gold. Marie had caught a whiff of something exotic, sweet and tangy, like nothing she has smelled before. Vira had replaced the wrapping and tucked the pouch away in his shirt. He had torn the piece in two and offered her half, signalling broadly for her to eat it. She had been wary until he popped his own fragment in his mouth and closed his eyes. She had followed suit only to find that it was some kind of dried fruit, something she had never tasted before. Like the fragrance, it was sweet and tangy, with layers of flavour bursting and rolling in over her tongue, against the inside of her cheeks, in the farthest crevices of her mouth. She doesn't think she has tasted anything so strange, so foreign, so complete.

The taste still lingered in her mouth when she had asked him how long till his unit left for the front. They were giggling like children as she tried to make him understand the question, waving and pointing north, holding up her arms as if cradling a rifle and making booming sounds. Vira had held up both hands, lifting each finger until all ten were straight.

Marie had nodded and then hopped off the wall to lead Vira by the hand into the cottage. Ten days were enough for her to learn how a man's touch felt when she

31

wished for it. And she had liked knowing that up close Vira's eyelashes were long and thick like a girl's and that she could see his cheeks flush red even under his oak-gold skin.

They had not eaten the porridge until much later in the night, after they had explored each other, after Vira had whispered many indecipherable words in her ear, after Marie had learned that she was capable of sighs and moans and pleasure she had never imagined.

Vira had come to her every afternoon in the next days. She would find him waiting patiently on the garden wall when she returned from gathering her supplies. They would sit in silence until he would pull out the oilcloth pouch, withdraw his precious hoard of the golden dried fruit and ration out a single piece that he'd tear in half to share with her. Marie would take the lead with the first kiss, mingling the tang of the strange fruit on their tongues and leading him into the cottage and to her bed. The next morning, he would be gone and she would discover small gifts: plant beds hoed, weeds cleared, wood chopped and added to the pile.

They never had the ten days that Vira had promised. On the eighth day, he had come before dawn, tapping frantically on the single windowpane till she had awakened. He had held her hands and explained, waving to the north over and over again. He had pointed to his bare wrist and then the sky repeatedly until Marie understood that his unit was leaving within hours. He had pulled out the oilskin pouch and halved a piece of the golden fruit and then raised her share to her lips. He had kissed her while the sweetness still lingered on her lips and then pushed the pouch into her hands. As he had backed away, he had smiled and tucked his half into his shirt pocket.

* * *

Marie considers the jars of roots and leaves and flowers. Not the ones that sit on her shelves but those she hides in the hollow under the floorboard. She has waited for news from the front for weeks, has resolutely ignored the stories that filter back south. At the market, they speak of the courage of the soldiers from the east. She tries not to listen to stories of the massacres, of casualties, of the sheer numbers that have perished in the fields of war.

She suspected when she did not bleed after Vira left. She was certain even before the news of the battles arrived, but waited for word of him even as the time for tea passed. Her fingers linger over the knitting needle nestled in a fold of clean muslin as her other hand caresses her swelling belly. The time for the needle will pass soon too, unless she wishes to risk pain, even death.

Finally, she turns to the oilcloth pouch on the table. She raises it slowly, opens it just a little. She closes her eyes and takes a single deep breath, filling her nose with the rich aroma. She had chosen herself once before, with Vira. She smiles as she closes the pouch and chooses herself again.

* * *

Four harvests had passed when the stained, crumpled letter arrived at Wazir Singh's home in Pathankot. Even more had passed when the regiment returned with too many missing. Those who did return were grim-faced and bleak-eyed. They talked of poisoned air and terrible weapons that ripped men to scraps, and whispered of battles without honour, of apocalypse brought by war machines, of horrors that leached the bravest man's courage.

Since then, the fields have been planted and harvested again and again. But Wazir Singh hopes still, even as the ink fades and the yellowed paper melts a little more each day under his fingertips. And he holds his son Vira's words to his heart: "The women of France are kinder than the memsahibs. Their smiles keep us warm even in this wretched cold and the sweetest of them open to us like flowers to the sun."

Each day, as the sun dips behind the western hills, Wazir Singh prays that his Vira rests in the arms of a kind woman of France and not in its blood-soaked soil.

Diplomatic Immunity Fatigue

I suppose the trouble began when JP and I met Lucy, or at least the trouble began for Lucy. And I suppose we should feel responsible for what followed. But frankly, if it hadn't been for the dead attaché, we wouldn't have met her, we wouldn't have even gotten to be friends, and then she would have gone on to one of those posh colleges and married some rich bastard as the rest of her lot do. But you know something? I sure don't feel responsible, and if someone should take the rap, well, blame it on those cloak-and-dagger games that governments play.

I suppose I should start with the dead military attaché. In truth, none of us was particularly surprised to learn that the kidnapped diplomat had turned up dead. We all kind of grew up with the idea that diplomats are fairly easily sacrificed pawns in the dirty tricks games everyone likes to call international politics. I mean, you try to keep your lot safe and alive, but if a few get knocked off, well, things happen you know. Nature of the game and all that! I suppose we were all geo-strategy cynics by the time we hit puberty anyway.

It was an evening like any other: my parents bathed the baby, while my sister and I watched television. "Could you bring me an extra towel," my mum called out, sticking her head out of the bathroom. That was the code.

All our family conversations happened in the bathroom, with urgent whispers, as the taps ran full blast and my baby brother squealed and splashed in the water. The joys of living in a bugged house! Lucky that he enjoyed water – he must have been the single most bathed kid in the world. It's probably good for national security that he also enjoyed high places and posing for the camera from the moment he could sit up on his own – that kid spent his childhood being photographed against strategic installations. Yes, bomb the spot where the kid is positioned! I can just imagine some hotshot general using a red laser pointer, tracing the nuclear power plant in the background, and triangulating the target from my baby brother smiling in the corner.

We all knew there had been another diplomat kidnapped and killed just months before. And strange nebulous threats were emanating nearly daily from shadowy groups against diplomatic staff from all sorts of nations. The only rule seemed to be that if your country wasn't the one paying for them to go kill, you made a fair target.

There would be restrictions on all our movements, Dad continued whispering, as my mum tried to keep my brother making as much noise as possible. In real terms that meant we were stuck hanging out at the various embassy pools, or in somebody's home, all of which with adult supervision. "Oh, and no driving around," Dad hissed. Great! The one thing in this boring, dead town that gave us a buzz! As far as I could see, international geo-strategy was ruining my social life forever.

I knew arguing wouldn't work. Security was one thing the family didn't argue about, no matter how ridiculous the restrictions got – and they did get absurd at times, like when the watchers trailed my sister's tricycle all the way from our house to the neighbourhood kindergarten three doors down. In a black car with tinted windows! Besides, it would take too long, and Mum wasn't going to let the baby turn into a prune, just to discuss my social life, which as far as I could see was going to hell in a CIA-paid bucket.

So a few days later when my father asked me accompany him to the SOS Village fundraising do, of course I said yes. Anything's better than watching yet another imported beach rescue programme on the television, especially when they cut out all the scenes with women in bikinis. Why men in tiny shorts are okay, I don't understand, but then that's idiots for you. If you watch the Bond flicks, pirated out of Moscow, they cut out all the bits with flashy cars! You grow up around us lot and all films are like moving puzzles, with different bits cut out by different countries. Once we did a *Moonraker* night with eight versions – funny how no two had the same bits taken out. That's geopolitics for you, I guess.

I knew the dinner would be a dead bore. These things always are: a coalition for saving some random country, or talking about how the mujahideen were doing such a good job, or whatever. One of those things that the Americans or Europeans throw together every so often to make themselves look multilateral, and for everyone else to make information runs.

It was one of those dreadful evenings that my father dragged me to whenever my mum was out of town or just busy with the baby. Not because he loved my scintillating seventeen-year-old company, but rather because he needed someone to clear a DLB in the ladies' toilet. I never understood that you know? Why set up a drop when you know you can't physically enter the ladies' without attracting attention? Anyway, it was pretty routine: I took all of three minutes to check the back of the cistern and pull out the piece of paper taped there. Then of course we had to kill time because you can't just walk in and out of these do's.

I started talking to Lucy partly because I was bored, and she was at least closer to my age than the rest of the place, and partly because the champagne was making my nose tickle. And if I didn't start talking, the bubbles would start making me sneeze. Not a good look that. She was the earnest type – brought along by her mother, one of those major philanthropists who ran charitable projects in obscure countries that would have been happier taking more of her money and less of her ideas. You know the kind. With slightly scared eyes, perfectly styled hair, and expensive clothes that looked just a bit too old for her. Probably the sort that never quite felt comfortable in her own skin. I still don't know if I spoke to Lucy only because I was bored, or because she had a weird Bambi look to her, you know the wide-eyed, scrubbed clean, kind that you makes you want to kick her teeth in.

Lucy was real money, with a father that made way too much of it, doing all sorts of shit even though she said he did oil. She went to one of the private schools where everyone looks the same, not like our rainbow coalition international school, and where everyone takes vacations in remote peaceful places to ski or surf or something, instead of going home once a year for a refresher course in national cultures. And she was the idealist sort anyway – campaigning for starving kids in Africa, mistreated women in inner-city neighbourhoods, even telling her mother that she wasn't going to wear fur as she supported

PETA. Like properly not wear fur – unlike the rest of her gang, who just ensured they wouldn't get spray-painted or laughed at and so wore mink-lined bomber jackets instead. No, Lucy was properly idealistic. Even the damn do had been organised by her mother, one of those flashy rich wives that go around saving the world that their husbands fuck up. And Lucy had actually helped. Can you believe that?

I guess it was always going to be bad news when we became friends. My lot were not only not proper money, we were also cynics from the age of five. We had grown up with diplomatic immunity – which meant we drank before anyone else did (although quality stuff that our parents stocked), drove way over the speed limit despite being underage, in cars with diplomatic plates and never pulled over for a cop. And worse still, we never got dewy-eyed about how the world would change because we worked so hard for it. I mean we all knew that warlords and drug-runners were bad, but shit, we all knew at least one who made it to our parent's guest list at dinner.

Poor Lucy – she never stood a chance. With the new security detail, the only bit of fun to be had – not counting getting high on the shit that JP sourced – was to shock and scare the daylights out of her: the first night she came to mine, JP (from a since defunct nation-state) had just rocked up with a Pashtun-made pistol. We played Russian roulette for a while – didn't tell her, of course, that we had taken out all the bullets. I mean, hell, one thing growing up in the service teaches is you is how to survive! You had to see her face when she held the barrel to her perfect little blonde head. You could make a million bucks of that if you made a film of it. The rest of us nearly killed ourselves laughing.

And god, she was an innocent. "But that's drugs," she gasped as I demonstrated how to make fruit salad with extra honey and about five hundred mixed up pills powdered in Mum's Moulinex. JP nearly pissed himself laughing about it later that night. But then, that may just have been the effect of the pills.

Unlike my parents, JP's were a bit oblivious to the shit he got up to. Or they just chose to look the other way while he raised all sorts of hell. Already by the age of sixteen, and less than three years after the Afghan war started, JP had a nice little business going on the side, all thanks to the diplomatic bag and friends in the army. His mates would pick up heroin from the source for dirt cheap and bring it over when they came out for leave. JP would collect it off them, spread a layer of it between a photograph glued to thick cardboard paper to look like a postcard, and send it off through the dip bag.

Hell, he must have written dozens of those postcards every week: "Dude, this village got air-bombed last week. "This is where the ambush happened. Took this pic last year, but they say most of it is now gone. "Hey man, hope the winter is going well up there. It's bloody thirty degrees already out here. Darling, can you send me some of that super-hold hair gel? Mine got shared out with the whole school." And so on and on . . . I suppose if you are going to run drugs small-time – even though JP said his operation was growing – you may as well use the dip bag. And then his friends at other posts would send back care packages, with bottles of hair gel with little plastic bags of pills inside. Heroin went out; Es, acid, whatever else Berlin, London and Paris was doing came in, and then up to his buddies up north. Wonder what the airports made of those drug-searching dogs going nuts at dip bags every week?

Trouble, as I said before, began when Lucy met JP. She thought he needed to be saved, and that she was the one to do it, just by helping him defect to a free country. He thought the business needed more cargo space and knew her dad had a private jet, and, well, JP was a better capitalist than Lucy would ever make. So before you knew it, Lucy was in love, and JP's little sideline had grown into a proper business. He and I sounded out other friends who had moved away, locating them at a few dozen embassies of a couple of dozen countries. Good thing about growing up like us, you know people everywhere. JP's little sideline kept growing, what with Lucy agreeing to carry presents – crates of mangoes, old brass lamps, onyx sculptures – to friends in Amsterdam and New York and Montreal. And of course, she brought back all sorts of stuff for JP – especially videotapes of American flicks that his friends would prepare for him, the fat plastic cases packed tight with pills and other shit. If I were a romantic, I would say they were a match made in heaven. Except that they left a used condom behind our sofa one afternoon, and I got not only grounded forever but also repatriated right back home for school. So god help me if I don't feel terribly sentimental about their love story.

JP never did defect, you know. He would have been stupid to do so. His grand-dad was a big shot back at internal intel, and when the country fell apart, there was lots of business to take care of, and money to be made, and JP was right in the middle of it. The last time our paths crossed, it was in central Africa a couple of years ago. He had a jet of his own by then, was running quantities of shit of all kinds.

We had dinner one night – all grown-up – just me, JP, and some tinpot genocidal loon with diamonds to pay for guns, who had been friends, back in the day, with my dad. We drank too much, laughed ourselves sick, and then toasted to remaining alive. Which is a whole hell of a lot more than Lucy managed. Apparently she went home with a broken heart, for losing JP or not getting him to defect we shall never know. She apparently did the whole It-girl routine for a few years till she walked off the balcony of her 23rd-floor penthouse one night.

She must have been feeling nostalgic, as apparently they found enough E in her system to keep a battalion happy, along with antidepressants and god knows what else. Poor kid – she never did get over spiked fruit salads. Oh well, collateral damage, I guess.

Number-nine Bungalow

Death came silently, frequently, to the little town in the mountains. And it always chose the men. They would go away on mysterious journeys, on "operations", carrying olive-green rucksacks and holding rifles black and glistening with oil, like a schoolgirl's plaits. Fingers caressed prayer beads, lips moved soundlessly over the sacred words, and eyes looked steadily forward, as the trucks carried them away.

Left behind, the women would watch the soldiers disappear into the distance. And a little later, the hum of a plane would rise from the distant airstrip. The women would pause in their conversations, their prayers, their cooking, to listen to the drone grow softer as the aeroplane flew far, far away.

Theirs was a small community, spread over a mountainside, dotted with bungalows that the British had built nearly a century ago. Lower down the slopes were the barracks, and still lower, and closest to the plains, was the tiny market. Beyond the tall deodar tops, the mountainside dipped into a wide valley, the Doon valley with its soil rich with fragrant basmati scents.

On clear nights, the lights twinkled right across the valley and onto the mountains at its other end, like a sparkling necklace flung carelessly across the darkness. That end, where the sirens never called for blackouts, was Mussoorie, a tourist town. A happy, social town, full of parties and laughter. Even as a seven-year-old, Ruchi knew, when she watched the Mussoorie lights, that Death went infrequently to that far town. Because Death stayed right here in the cantonment, stalking over the misty mountaintop high above the bungalows, amongst the multi-coloured prayer flags. It sneaked past the offices where the "operations" were planned; crept past the cheerful barracks that smelt of butter tea, thukpa and momos. Death climbed silently onto the olive-green trucks that carried the men away on operations. It stowed away secretly on the aeroplanes that flew the men even farther than the Doon valley below.

Ruchi knew this, because when the men returned, grim and weary, there would be faces missing from their ranks. "Death marched again with us," her father, unshaven and bone-tired, would inform her mother as he collapsed on the soft bed, too weary even to remove his mud-spattered jungle boots. Mother would look grave, sometimes even weep a little, as she removed Father's boots and then tucked him safe under the vast green down quilt.

When Death took the officers, their passing would be marked with a quick, sombre toast in the mess, and by the hasty removal of the dead man's family down to the plains. In the barracks, the passing was even quieter. A face would vanish, only to be replaced by another, impassive one, even as the other soldiers continued their chanting: "Om mani padme hum."

* * *

On days that Father was not away on operations, he took Ruchi for walks on the mountainside. They would stroll through the deodars, the rhododendrons and the pines on the higher reaches. Ruchi's favourite stretch was a solitary walk lined with towering pine trees where the ground was carpeted by tangy-smelling needles that sank beneath her feet. In the dim twilight that always lived under the tall trees, Father taught her to walk silently, testing the twigs and needles under her soft-soled shoes. "Not a crack," he would instruct, solemnly demonstrating his own stealth. Later, kneeling on the pine needles in companionable silence, they would watch the clouds swirl through the narrow gaps in the mountains and observe the creatures of the forest go about their own business.

Once, while walking on that soft pine carpet, Ruchi found a small furry body the colour of dry dirt. A faint, acrid smell rose from it. "Death marched with it," Father murmured, running his fingers through her hair. They moved away, Father carrying her home in his arms. From the edge of their garden overlooking the pine walk, Ruchi heard him instruct one of the soldiers. "Bury the body, pinja-la, I don't want her upset again."

Later, when Father had gone up to the offices near the top of the hill, Ruchi ran back down to the pine walk to see the animal again. The body was already gone and the patch covered with a fresh layer of sharp, green needles. But the odour – of the non-living – still lingered on the spot, blending with the tangy new scent of the needles.

* * *

When she grew older, Ruchi could never remember how she came to identify Number-nine bungalow as Death's house. Perhaps, Gompo-la, the sweet-tempered soldier-monk who watched over her as she played, had informed her. Or perhaps Father told her about the abandoned old house that stood not a half-kilometre from their own, a faded number 9 painted in black on its rickety wooden gate.

Its red roof was of the same corrugated metal as the other bungalows. Its wide veranda had the same dark wood floorboards. The front of the house had a large picture window, with square glass panes set in an ornate rosewood frame. But unlike the other bungalows, the paint was peeling off the yellowed walls, the red on the roof was faded. Even the rosewood window frames didn't shine with fresh polish. The pebbled path leading up to the front door was overgrown with weeds. The garden was tangled and wild. The rosebushes were gnarled and twisted with age, and the wild irises flashed a startlingly bright blue in the tall grass.

She did, however, remember the first time she walked up to the Number-nine bungalow, with Father. They had gone to the house for cloud-catching.

The clouds on the mountains never came low enough to enter their home. Instead, they swirled and twisted and blanketed the mountaintop with a foamy pearl-grey. "We are too low, Ruchi," Father would explain patiently. On such days, when the mountaintop was hidden by the clouds, Father would take her up there and let her run through the prayer flags. She would race through the pennants, tasting the moisture on her tongue, trailing cloud-phantoms at the tips of her fingers. She would run through the clouds, letting the damp, wispy, yet opaque streams hide her. And then, she would wait for Father to find her. "Ruchi," Father would call, striding through the translucence, cutting through the mists. "Ruchi," he would call again, laughter audible in his voice. And then,

Sunny Singh

suddenly, he would appear through the clouds, large and solid amidst the vapours, like a hero, or a god. His hair would be slick and shiny with moisture, his cheeks chilled by the mountain air. Laughing, he would swoop down to gather her up, his clothes damp and cold, but his arms would be warm around her as he marched steadily through the clouds.

But Ruchi wanted to trap the clouds. To catch them in the house and keep them forever. She wanted to open the windows to let the clouds come into the rooms. And then quickly, very quickly, just when they had filled up the rooms, she would close the windows. And the clouds would have to stay in the house for her to play with, whenever she wanted.

When Ruchi explained her plan to Father, he laughed. But once he stopped laughing, he patted her head. "A good plan, a very good plan. Just like a guerrilla's. You are learning fast."

"So I can go on operations with you soon?" Ruchi immediately asked. That was the whole point of showing Father that clouds could be caught; that her tactics were as good as any officer's; that she was ready to be a guerrilla like the pinja-las.

"Hmm, soon! Let me see. I think you have to be a little taller to be a guerrilla," Father solemnly informed her, examining her closely, holding his palm a little above her head, the height he explained was necessary to be a

50

guerrilla. "But we should test your plan for trapping the clouds," he told her, noting the disappointment on her face. "It is a very good plan. We won't hold them forever, but just as a test. For a little while only. Yes?"

The only hitch, of course, was that their own home was too low for the clouds to reach. The only house in town high enough to lure them was Number-nine bungalow. Death's bungalow.

Father said that he would find the right moment to take her up to the bungalow. Ruchi knew he was watching for a time when Death had gone walking elsewhere. Then they would sneak into the empty house and work at cloud-catching.

It was many days later that Father decided the time was right. The sky was dark and when he walked with Ruchi through the deodars, the wind blew fierce and cold, sucking away her breath and stinging her cheeks.

Hand in hand, they approached the gaping, blind windows. The glass panes were dirty and dim, but no curtains hid the empty insides. As Ruchi placed her foot on the first wooden step to the veranda, the board creaked. She froze immediately, holding her breath. Father smiled at her, pointing to his own feet that stepped cunningly, silently on the same boards. She nodded, shifting her weight carefully so as not to make a sound with her next step. The front door was bolted but not locked. When Father tugged at the bolt, it squealed loudly. Ruchi's heart gave a lurch. What if the sound had warned Death? But Father just smiled at her, and that reassured her.

Once inside, Father and Ruchi sped through the rooms, flinging the windows open. Latches protested, frames creaked, but they continued opening the windows to the winds. Father pointed out of the picture window. "Look, they are on their way down." Ruchi turned her head to see the clouds roll down from the top of the mountain. Like spreading rolls of silk, or a flood, the clouds made their way towards them, covering the tall pines and deodars. Steadily, almost imperceptibly, the first translucent fingers would reach to caress a tree, then slowly wrap themselves around the green heights. And moments later, the tree would be invisible, hidden in the voluminous grey blanket. Watching the clouds make their way inexorably through the forest, Ruchi felt a sudden flash of terror. A cold, wet finger ran fleetingly down her spine, raising the soft hairs on the back of her neck. Her breath caught in her throat. Suddenly the clouds seemed sinister, portending evil in a way they never had on the mountaintops.

Beside her, Father laughed, throwing back his head. "We'll catch them alright." Ruchi had a sudden vision of the mysterious operations he went away for where the enemy approached, much like the clouds, vast and strong and dangerous. And in the trees, hidden with the pinja-las, the gleaming rifles loaded and ready, her father laughing in anticipation.

That cold wet finger on her spine, Ruchi realised, in a flash of frighteningly adult clarity, was her fear for her father. It was her first experience of the terror that all those who love a soldier must learn to bear. Death marched with her father too, and at any moment, in any place, could swoop down to claim him. She felt tears prick her eyes, even as the clouds reached the house, swirling gently against the peeling yellowed walls.

"Stay here," Father commanded, laughter still in his voice. "I'll go close the windows." Ruchi could only make a soft sound, a clutching sob that ripped at her throat, as Father moved away. She reached out after him but caught only a damp wisp. The clouds had already started crowding Death's bungalow, pushing through the window like unruly children at recess.

Ruchi was blinded by the billowing opacity, but she still could hear Father closing the windows, bolting each one carefully. She strained to hear his footsteps, but he walked as always on soundless feet. Time seemed to have halted, and nothing moved in the clouds that had filled the bungalow. She held out her hands before her and could only vaguely make out their outline. She stared blindly into the damp around her and felt terror clutch at her heart. Tears poured now, running freely down her cheeks. Her hands were cold and clammy with the moisture from the clouds. She rested her head against the rosewood window frame, finding solace in its solidity, and sobbed uncontrollably.

She was still staring blankly before her when a silent figure loomed over her. The shoulders were massive, the head dark. It leaned out to pull one of the panels of the picture window shut. Ruchi held her breath, hoping it wouldn't notice her. Then the figure seemed to search for something; dark, slim-fingered hands running over the rosewood. She hid in her corner, shrinking into herself in fear. Oh, if only Father would return!

As the hands moved closer, she shut her eyes, squeezing them tightly. She screamed when she felt the hand touch her shoulder. "No!"

Then suddenly, she was in Father's arms, cradled against his chest. "What frightened you, baby? It's alright, everything is alright," he murmured against her hair. His lips felt her cheeks, passing over the tears and the moisture the clouds had left. "Shhh, it's alright." He carried her home just like that, with her head nestled under his chin, her body pressed tight against his chest. She could feel his pulse throbbing in his throat against her face and pressed her cheek up to its rhythm. He is alive, he is still alive, she exulted, breathing in his scent – musky and tangy like the forest. She knew she was echoing the words in her mind that she had heard her mother whisper each time Father came home. They were a chant, a sacred chant, like *Om mani padme hum*. Suddenly, she knew what the words meant, why the pinja-la chanted them as they went on operations. "He is alive, he is still alive."

And the first inkling of a plan began to form in her head, as she pressed herself closer still to Father. She would imprison Death; leave him locked in his Number-nine bungalow before Father left again on operations. She would make sure that Death would never march again with the soldiers.

* * *

The day before Father left on operations, he always spoke to Ruchi separately. The words were different each time, but the message was always the same. They would go down to the shaded pine walk, hand in hand, treading carefully on the needles. "You must take care of Mother. She worries too much, so you must be brave and take care of her so she can worry less." Ruchi always nodded seriously and held Father's hand tighter.

The night before Father left, there was always a big dinner with all his favourite dishes. And Mother made a special treat: ice cream packed with raisins, wild berries picked from the bushes on the slope and shreds of sweet plum from the tree in the garden. The three of them would sit together over dinner, talking softly about unimportant things such as a new doll for Ruchi, or Mother's need for a new pressure cooker. Sitting up so late, Ruchi would almost fall asleep on the table. Unlike other days, she wasn't told to go to bed.

Late in the night, Father would tuck her under the heavy down quilt. He would stroke her forehead softly and kiss her cheek. Ruchi knew that on nights before he left, Father stayed up even later to talk to Mother. She would lie half-asleep in her bed, listening to the murmurs, the rustling of sheets and the incomprehensible, hushed moans that came from her parents' room. At some point, as she tried to make sense of the sounds, she would fall asleep.

In the morning, when she awoke, Father would have already left. Which was why she needed to carry out her Death-trapping plan before he took her for a stroll to the pine walk. She had already heard the whispers, listening in secretly to the things that grown-ups said at dinners in the officers' mess when they thought that the children could not hear:

"High casualties on the eastern sector ... four companies decimated ... full out war this time ... Major Rai and his boys just cut down at the dam ... poor Mrs. Rajan, after only one month of the wedding, he has been sent on ops ..."

Mother had already told her that Father would be gone for longer than usual. "This time, the operations will last a long time, Ruchi. But maybe we will go down to the plains and see your cousins. We can even go to Nani's house." Mother had tears in her eyes as she said this, and Ruchi knew that Death would march with Father and his men on these operations. But she wouldn't let that happen.

For days she watched carefully the lock on the big trunk under the bed. It was the only lock in the house, a big shiny yellow circle with a dull steel handle and its key – on a large round ring with lots of other keys – stayed in the top drawer of the high mahogany dresser in her parents' bedroom. She had tried to take the shiny brass key for the lock off the ring that held so many other keys together, but the whole bunch was very heavy and loud, clanking with every movement. But the ring was tight, its spirals almost impossible to prise apart. In the end, she took the whole bunch, deciding to return it after she had locked Death in.

Removing the lock from the trunk under the bed had been easier. Mother knew that Ruchi often played under the bed and never disturbed her. "She is afraid," Mother had told Father. "It is this uncertainty all around." But the lock was heavy, making her arms ache when she carried it – gripped with both hands – up the mountain. The keys clanged loudly in her pocket.

"Baba, where are you going?" Gompo-la called after her. She nearly cried in frustration at being spotted. He caught up with her easily, loping after her with his long stride. For a moment, she hesitated.

"To Number-nine bungalow," she whispered, unable to lie to the concerned face above her.

Gompo-la was surprised. "But no one goes there, Ruchi-baba."

"Oh, I know," she declared airily, trying to hide the lock behind her back. Gompo-la had already seen it. He didn't ask any more questions. Instead, he squatted down before her, balancing on the balls of his feet, waiting for her explanation. Ruchi stared at him, wondering if he would laugh at her, or worse, stop her from carrying out her plan.

Finally, she decided. "I am going to lock Death in the house. Then he can't march with the soldiers tomorrow. It's a secret, and you have to help me."

Gompo-la seemed surprised. But he didn't laugh. Or even ask any more questions. He nodded wisely, his narrow eyes suddenly shiny and moist. "In the old days, in Tibet, we did the same. Before a war, the lamas locked away all the evil spirits. Come, I will help you."

So, they walked hand in hand up to Number-nine bungalow. Gompo-la volunteered to go and find out if Death was indeed home. As he sneaked through the garden, Ruchi watched the silent house. Its windows were bolted shut again. From a distance, she thought she saw a shadow move inside. Scared, she huddled down further, clutching the lock tightly.

Then Gompo-la came back. "Yes, he is inside. Give me the lock. I will go put it on the door." He held out his hand. But she shook her head. Only she knew the secret words. Or rather the meaning of the sacred words that had to be said after she locked Death in.

"No, I have to put the lock myself."

Gompo-la nodded again, his eyes shining brightly. "Good officer always does first what he asks the jawans to do," he said, stepping aside.

Ruchi rose slowly to her feet, inching forward towards the house. Before her, the silent bungalow loomed large and frightening. The sun glinted off the windowpanes and she wondered if Death had seen her approach. The pebbles rolled and crunched under her feet, and the weeds scratched her bare legs as she forced herself to walk steadily up to the front door.

Once she stumbled as she walked. She put her hands out before her to break her fall. The lock was heavy and crushed her fingers as she hit the ground. There would be scratches, but when she looked down at her hands, there was no blood. One of them had touched a scorpion-grass plant, however, and began to itch. She felt tears well up in her eyes and forced herself not to wipe them. The poisonous grass would make her eyes burn too if she touched them.

She looked back and Gompo-la was still crouching on the ground beyond the garden. He smiled at her and motioned her forwards, swinging his right arm in a high, wide arc. She nodded and gathered her courage. She would tolerate the itching and pain until she got back. Then Gompo-la would find the plants to take the hurt away.

The first step up to the veranda began to creak before she remembered what Father had taught her. She removed her foot gently and then slowly replaced it, shifting her weight to tread silently. Slowly, quietly, almost holding her breath, she climbed up to the veranda.

Then swiftly stepping across the wide floorboards, she reached the door. Fumbling, nearly dropping the lock, she struggled to place it on the loop of the bolt. The door shook suddenly, banging against the frame, pulling away from her hands. Was someone trying to open it from the inside? She started, her heart beating wildly, and half-turned to run away. But then, she steadied herself, reaching for the bunch of keys in her pocket.

Concentrating fiercely, she found the shiny brass key, the only one in the bunch of its colour, and managed to fit it into the lock. "Om mani padme hum," she chanted under her breath, using all the strength in her arms to twist the key in the slot. The key was stuck and refused to move. She jiggled it back and forth, tugging at it, struggling to turn it. Finally, Ruchi felt the lock click shut. She tugged at it once, twice, before removing the key. For an instant, it caught in the lock again, and she had to twist it before it snapped free.

Triumphant, she turned, holding the bundle of keys up for Gompo-la to see. He jumped up and waved and laughed. She thought she knew how Father felt when his operations were over. Taking a deep breath, stifling the urge to run away from the house, she climbed steadily down the steps and walked through the garden and out onto the path. "Well done, baba, well done," Gompo-la shouted. As she drew closer, he smiled at her solemnly and stuck out his hand. Ruchi took it in hers, shaking it as she had seen Father do with his officers.

"Thank you for your help on this mission, Gompo-la," she intoned her father's words, mimicking his tone.

Gompo-la smiled and nodded, a different gesture this time. It was a crisp duck of the head, an almost-salute that the guerrillas used to acknowledge each other. Then, he bent down and put his hands on her shoulders. "Very good," he announced, looking solemnly, deeply, into her eyes. Ruchi was glad that his hands were strong because her legs shook with pent-up fear and relief. He smelled different from Father, of sweat and cigarettes and of cooked meats from the kitchen. For a long moment, he stared at her, his eyes narrow and inscrutable. Then, releasing her shoulders, he rose, stepped back, and clicked his heels together. She looked up to see his wide grin.

Without a word, she held out her hands to him and he leaned over to inspect them, noting the red itchy rash that had sprung up on her fingers. "No problem. Behind our house there are plants that will stop the itching. You will be tip-top by the time we reach home," he announced.

When she looked up at him, he was smiling. She laughed out loud, joyously, relieved; a laugh so infectious that he joined in. And so, laughing, they began their walk back down the mountain.

* * *

When Ruchi awoke the next morning, Father had left on operations. She ate her breakfast in silence and then found a seat on the veranda, the place where she always sat to wait for his return. She knew it would be some days before Father came home, but she watched the road twisting down the hill anyway. And softly, under her breath, she chanted.

The sun was high in the sky when Gompo-la came, having finished his chores, and sat on the steps, next to her stool. They smiled at each other conspiratorially. Watching the road together, they began to chant the sacred words, the words of hope:

Om mani padme hum!
He is still alive. He is still alive.
Om mani padme hum . . .

The Tigress Hunts

When the soldiers came to the village, I was playing at the well, just where the fields begin, trying to wait till the sun disappeared behind the trees before going home. Of course, Amma would scold me when I returned. "One day a ghost will get you. Don't you know they look for young girls like you. And just at the time when the sun is going away," she always threatened. But she still sent Dhanu-akka to find me every evening.

That afternoon, I started running home when I first heard the screaming. But someone caught me by just the end of my half-sari, and pulled me into the paddy.

"Shhh . . . quiet." It was Chitti, pushing me into the muddy waters even as I struggled to get away. She held me down in the paddy, nearly drowning me in the brown swamp, her hand pressed tight against my

63

mouth. She threw herself over me, pushing me further into the mud.

We stayed like that all night, with Chitti lying on top of me, nearly squeezing all the air out of me. The water in the field was cold and the ground was soft and squishy. But even though my fingers and toes felt like they would fall off with the cold, Chitti kept my back warm. She lay stiff over me, barely moving, her hand covering my mouth.

* * *

The soldiers left before dawn, but Chitti waited till the sun was high and hot before rolling off me. "See if you can move your arms and legs a bit," she whispered, showing me how to bring life back to my stiff limbs. Little tingles ran up my body as I tried to imitate her. Still, she had to pull me up by my arms to get me out of the mud, and we squished and squelched when we finally moved. Even then we stayed for a long time, crouching in the paddy, until Chitti decided it was safe to go back to the house.

We walked silently, in the shadows, pausing frequently against walls and behind trees, before we reached the narrow lanes of the village. Chitti went first, craning her neck around the corners of houses before running to the next turn. She held my hand tight and dragged me along. Away from the paddy, the mud dried on us, sticking to my hair, clumping up in the braids that Amma had made yesterday. Oh, Amma would be so angry, I kept thinking, she had just washed and oiled my hair the morning before. The mud caked my skin, fading on my arms like a light crust. I could feel it stretch the edges of my face as it dried.

Our house was empty. The kolam that Dhanu-akka made every morning had been rubbed away from the door. The kitchen fire was dead, the ashes cold and still. All of Amma's pots and pans were broken and overturned. In the corner, where Amma kept grain from the fields, there was nothing. All the sacks were gone. Only handfuls of rice remained scattered all over the floor.

I saw them first. Amma and Dhanu-akka. Lying near the hand pump. Some blood around them, mostly near the head. Hands and legs spread out. Dhanu-akka lay half-turned on her side, her legs spread out in strange angles, one arm flung across her middle. But Amma's breasts lay baking in the sun, floppy and empty, the nipples large and brown, encrusted with something darker. There was blood also between their legs. More on Dhanu-akka than on Amma. And on their bellies. The earrings that Appa had given her were gone from Amma's ears. Bits of flesh hung from the lobe, with streaks of blood marking the soft skin where her dark hair ended. I must have watched them for a long time, wondering if I should cover them.

Then Chitti pulled me away. Jerking me away from Amma, from Dhanu-akka, into her own slumped shoulders. She held me there for a long time, her arm wrapped tight around my head. "Ay, no, no, no," she kept mumbling, half-slumped against the wall. I peeped up at her face, twisting my own a little. Tears were streaming down her dark cheeks, washing slim rivers in the drying mud. "No, no . . . what to do now . . . ay, no, no, no."

We stood there for a long time, I think, my face crushed against Chitti's muddy sari. But finally she let me go. I didn't cry then, not even a tear. My eyelashes were crusted with the dried mud and I could barely see clearly. When I rubbed my hands across them, little clumps of mud came off, flecked with black, string-like lashes.

We left for the forest, quickly, not even pausing to gather things. Chitti just scraped up the scattered rice to tie at the end of her sari. Then we went, heading north to where soldiers couldn't reach us. Chitti didn't know the way but we kept going deep into the dark jungle, looking for places where the tigers stay. Places that could be safe, she told me. Tigers were safer than soldiers. Tigers would eat you up, but not leave you in your house, naked and bleeding, staring with blank dead eyes at the sun.

At first we hid, walking through the night and sleeping in the fields in the daytime. Many times we slept in the paddy, like on that first night. Me lying in the muddy waters, cold and shivering, with Chitti lying over me, suffocating me with her fleshy body that had smelt then of jasmine and coconuts. But now she smelled of dirt and sweat, and fear, I think. Something rancid and rotting. I had to hold my face against her shoulder to breathe. Turning the other way meant that I risked ending up with a nose full of mud. Each night I curled my fingers into the folds of her sari, holding on to the fabric as if it were life itself.

At the edges of the forests of the north, we began seeing other people. People who watched us for hours, perhaps even days, before they approached. Serious-looking men with suspicion in their eyes. Silent women with shoulders drooping under an unseen weight. They spoke with Chitti in whispers, indicating the direction we should take with quick jerks of their heads, a fleeting squinting of their eyes. But steadily, slowly, gradually, the fear receded from our backs and we began to walk up straight.

And then, as we passed into the deep shadows of the jungle, we started travelling in the daytime, sleeping under the trees at night. Chitti would lean against a tree trunk, pulling a few broad leaves over us as shelter against the rain. She pulled my head against her shoulder, her arms wrapped tightly around my waist. And each night, she hummed old lullabies, the same ones I remembered Amma singing. "Dear darling daughter, remember me. Dearest darling daughter, cry for your mother when you are in the house of your in-laws. Dearest darling daughter, never forget me, the mother who loves you best."

Finally, we came to the camp. It was a place where many people lived, some in tents and houses made from bits of wood and tin. Others – new, like us – just huddled under trees. There, safe from soldiers, Chitti tried to make me cry. She told me stories about Amma and Dhanu-akka. And about Appa. And finally, she told me about the cavity search.

"It was when we went to the city to find your father. There was not enough to eat that year from the fields. And the postman brought no money from Appa. That was when the postman stopped coming to the village," she told me in raspy whispers, as we huddled under the banana leaves.

I didn't care. I have never seen a postman. No one sends us money or anything else.

"At the crossing to the main road was a post of soldiers. They were laughing and talking. And spitting. They were checking everyone who was going into the city. Or mostly everyone. They didn't look at the people in the cars so closely. But everyone on foot – poor people like us – they checked. All in the open – thrusting their hands up under the women's saris, pushing their hands in the blouses. Some women were weeping. Their men stood, glaring but silent, heads turned away, eyes looking down. No one could say anything to the soldiers. Your Amma and I wept in fear when we stood in line. Your Amma kept saying how it was good Dhanu had been left in the village with the neighbours. 'Good she doesn't have to see this, my daughter.'

"They didn't check us when our turn came. Just pushing barrels of their guns against our bellies, moving it against our saris. 'Ha ha, nothing much on these old hags. Not even breasts. Why? Did your man leave you because there is nothing for him to hold?' We just stayed silent, your Amma holding you close against her shoulders. But then one of them laughed. And he pulled you away. He put you on the table – right on top of a bunch of papers and other things – and unwrapped the shawl around you. He just spread your little legs apart. And started to push with his fingers. You cried and cried, screaming so loud. Your Amma was crying and shouting and begging too. 'Stop stop, you are hurting her. Please stop.' But the soldier kept pushing, in one hole then another. 'How do I know you aren't carrying messages? Or hiding a bomb there?' We begged and wept but he kept pushing. Finally he stopped and wiped his fingers on the shawl. 'You can take her,' he told your Amma. Then he turned away."

Chitti paused and looked at me. Waiting. Wishing that I would cry. But no tears fell from my eye. Not then, not afterwards. She slapped me then, across the face, first once. Then twice. Then again and again. "Cry. Please cry." She pleaded. But no tears fell. So she hugged me close and covered me with her sari, humming an old lullaby against my ear, as if she thought I was still a baby.

As we lay there, staring into the darkness, I remembered Amma telling me of the trip to the city. Of her terror that she would never find Appa. Of her fear that she would have to go back to the village with nothing to eat and no seeds for the next crop. But she did find Appa. He had been so happy to see them. And he had cursed the postman who never brought us the money he had been sending. Amma and Chitti stayed with him in the city, until Amma's fears for Dhanu-akka made her return to the village.

In that time in the city, Appa gave Amma her gold earrings – thick and chunky with little knobs that glittered when they caught the light. He had saved money and bought them for her many months ago. "I was going to bring them to you when I returned home, but this way is much better." And he took Amma to the market and bought two silk saris – one for Dhanu-akka, the colours of a peacock's tail, and one for me in pink and red. For our weddings. "I will bring more, when that day comes, but it is better to buy these now," he promised Amma.

Amma would show us the saris every night when we were growing up. To remind us of Appa who never returned from the city. He disappeared into the soldiers' prison soon after. And we had no photographs to remember his face. So every night, before we went to sleep, Amma would open the trunk in the corner of the room, and take out the saris for us. "The blue one for Dhanu, and the pink for the baby, he said," Amma would tell us, even though we already knew. The three of us would sit on the floor, holding the saris carefully, gently, in our laps. We would run our fingers over that soft, shiny cloth, trying in vain to picture the man who had bought them for us. Then, Amma would replace them in the trunk and kiss us goodnight.

The saris were gone! I suddenly remembered. Or left behind in the house. "Chitti, the saris? Appa's saris! Where are they?" I whispered. "They were in the trunk in the corner."

"The trunk was open. Nothing was in there," Chitti whispered back. "The soldiers must have taken them." In the darkness she ran her fingers under my eyes, along my cheeks, checking for tears. "Cry, my darling daughter, please cry," she whispered again and again, putting the tune of the lullaby to her words. But no tears fell. Not then, not ever.

* * *

Strange that I think of things from so long ago tonight. Chitti is dead. One of the bombs that fall from the planes killed her in the forest. Many others died also. No Tigers, of course. Tigers are too smart to be caught in the forest by bombs from the sky.

I am alone now. But I am not afraid. Not even of cavity searches, even though Chitti wept for me each time it happened. I think all men do those. The soldiers, the drunken ones at the camp, and even the Tigers. With their fingers and other things. It hurts each time but pain can be forgotten, if you try hard. If you think of something else. And then pain, even fear, fades away like the darkness at dawn.

* * *

I am a Tigress now. And I received the orders for my mission a week ago. That is why I came to the city. To acquire the kit, to prepare. And then to hunt.

Yesterday we walked to the shops, I and my team. We shopped for things that I would need – for a silk sari, and jewellery, and shoes also. At the sari shop, I bought a pink silk sari, with a red border. I no longer remember the sari Appa had sent for my marriage. It shouldn't matter, I know. After all, I was married two years ago, dressed in the black uniform. My thali hangs around my neck. A capsule on a black thread, to be used if the soldiers catch me. Like a husband, it will protect me. Better than a husband, I think, because it won't look away or hang its head in front of the soldiers.

So why should it matter what colour sari I wear tomorrow? But yesterday, at the shop, when I saw that pink and red . . . I imagined that it was the same sari, from the same shop where Appa had taken Amma so long ago. The fabric slides through my fingers, slippery and soft, like so much coconut oil. And we bought some pink embroidered sandals with shiny red, little heels. I will have to be careful when I walk in them tomorrow. I have never worn shoes with heels before.

At the jewellery shop we bought red-and-pink bangles. Shiny twinkling bands of glass with flecks of gold in them. And a pair of earrings – not gold, of course. Money is better spent on more important items of a hunter's kit. Still, they are golden with little knobs, and dangle from my ears. Wearing them was difficult at first and Aruna had to pull out the bits of wood from my lobes first. They left behind little strings of blood, but the earrings gleamed against my cheek. We giggled as we looked in the mirror, and she wiped away the blood from my ears with her sari.

I also bought a small pin at the jewellery shop. The first and only thing I have ever bought for myself. It is shaped like a golden butterfly, with wings of many colours, red, blue, green. On the back is a safety pin, like those we use for bandages. I will use it to hold my sari in place tomorrow, so it doesn't slip across my shoulders. And tomorrow I will look like a bride, ready for her marriage.

That is how we will reach the target. Dressed like a happy, pretty bride. Tomorrow, I will go to the hotel where soldiers gather to relax and eat and laugh. I will ask to meet my fiancé in the hotel meant only for the officers with ribbons of many colours on their chests, and gold stars on their shoulders.

And tomorrow, my companions will help me prepare. They will put the sandals with the shiny red heels on my feet. Aruna has already painted my toenails with bright pink paint. They will fasten the belt securely across my belly and breasts. I know I must be careful as I walk, and hold my head straight and high and not hold my arms too tight against myself. I know that I must smile, and walk slowly to the inside of the hotel. And I know that I have to be sure to bend slowly, slightly, when I detonate the explosives.

In other lands, a Tiger told us that the belt carries only enough explosives to leave the head intact. Afterwards, the head can be found and seen. And photographed and perhaps even prayed to. A Tigress's head is valuable even if it can't bite. So my belt will be loaded to leave no sign of me but the hunt.

Tomorrow the golden earrings will dangle in my ears. And I will wrap the pink and red silk around me like a shy new bride. There will be fresh jasmine in my hair, I know. Aruna has asked Anna to buy three strands in the morning from the flower seller in the market. And then the butterfly pin on my shoulder, just above the belt, to make sure my sari doesn't slip and slide off. No tears will fall tomorrow. Tomorrow, the Tigress will hunt . . .

The Wait

Mrs. Sharma waits for her husband to come home every day. Returning from the college where she teaches, she takes up her usual post on an easy chair on her veranda. The chair is placed to give her a clear view beyond the metal grill gate right up to the end of the street. She will see him when he turns up the street to walk towards the house.

When she looks back at her life, she has done nothing but wait. First, for her father's olive-green uniform and the toys he would bring her on his infrequent trips home. And then for the blue of her husband's Air Force colours. She married her husband because her father said that Air Force officers ran a lower risk of getting killed in battle. Back when the country was fighting three wars in a decade, these were considerations that mattered to a young girl of marriageable age.

But then the country went to war again. Soon after, the telegram arrived. Her husband wasn't dead though. Air Force officers don't die that frequently in battle. But he was missing, presumed taken prisoner. So she waited.

Then came liberation – of a country, of prisoners of war, of enemy soldiers in our jails. And still she waited. There was no liberation for her. Every day, she watches for that blue uniform to walk up the street, holding a bunch of flowers, or a bag of jalebis. Or even empty-handed. And she waits still, as she has every day, for the past thirty years.

* * *

Squadron Leader A. K. Sharma had allegedly escaped from the military prison that had been his home for the past thirty years. He had even apparently called the embassy, although no one could imagine how.

"If he tells me where he is, I will put him in my car and drive him across the border," L. "Matty" Mathan, formerly a captain in the Indian Army and presently the Consul Passport and Visas, at the Indian High Commission whispered to his wife.

"Will that be appropriate?" Anita's mouth was close against Matty's ear, her breath tickling the sensitive skin there. He felt an involuntary sexual response as they sat on the edge of the bathtub, the shower running behind them to hide the sounds of their conversation from the inevitable bugs.

"Probably not. Smashing through the border is probably an international incident, especially if you are driving a diplomatic car," Matty smiled wryly, slipping his arm around Anita's waist. "But he is a serviceman. Damn it, we even served in the same sector . . ." His whisper sounded loud.

Anita put her head on his shoulder. The phone call in the afternoon had revived memories she had buried deep inside: of Matty going to war, of standing in the doorway for interminable hours, of her stomach hollowing at the sight of every army jeep. The inevitable prayer, God don't let them stop at her house. And then the guilt when the solemn officer halted at a neighbour's house instead. She would wait for confirmation and then gather herself. Another soldier was dead. Another messenger of death had visited, leaving devastation in its wake. She, along with the other wives, would go to help clean up the debris. And Matty? Of daredevil reputation, and no news? She never expected a letter from him. Instead she scanned the casualty lists in the newspapers every morning, looking for friends and acquaintances. And almost casually, non-committally, for Matty.

Decades ago she had buried the guilt of seeing him home safe when so many others grieved still or waited. Buried that sour emotion deep under the joy and relief.

She had learned to soothe and calm, and only be afraid, alone, late at nights, when Matty lay breathing heavily, asleep next to her. Matty no longer went to war, she knew. Instead, they played childish games with listening devices and shower-muffled conversations. She doesn't mind whispering over the running water or loud music. Snuggled close, their cheeks rubbing together, hot breath rustling in their hair and caressing their ears, their practical conversations have the romance of furtive erotic interludes.

But a single phone call resuscitated the dead fears. War was back, and she could not keep Matty out of it.

With an effort, Anita calmed the butterflies in her stomach and slid her hand into Matty's. "I think you should start looking for another job. This will kill off your career completely." She smiled at her thin joke as Matty pulled her tight in his arms.

"Thank you," he whispered. "It could be a trap, of course."

"Because of the delegation that came? For the prisons?"

"Yes. And because Mrs. Sharma came for dinner here."

"But only for two hours. She needed her own people," Anita blurted, her voice rising in protest. Matty put his fingers on her lips.

"Yes, service people," she hissed. "After all, it's enemy territory. Looking for her husband after so long. How could they . . ." She trailed off.

She had known how to cope with the open war, where soldiers went off and never came back, where the enemy was identifiable and placed in clearly demarcated sectors, where the news of battles came on the radio, and casualty lists were published in the daily newspapers. But this new war she didn't understand. With bugs, and unofficial assaults, of kidnappings and secret tortures that didn't meet international conventions. She tried to remember what she could of that dinner with Mrs. Sharma.

She remembered the roly-poly woman who had come with a delegation of families to check the prisons. With grey streaks in her neatly bound hair and a cotton sari that seemed crumpled even at breakfast, Anita couldn't believe Mrs. Sharma was an army wife. Such a frump. Then she had caught a glimpse of the sad, droopy eyes and scolded herself for her thoughts. If Matty hadn't returned, she wondered, would she have grown into Mrs. Sharma too? Aged before her time? Ravaged?

Matty hadn't wanted her to meet the delegation. "I don't want you to be sad, Anita," he had told her over dinner. She had known he was right.

From Islamabad, Mrs. Sharma and the delegation had gone to Quetta, and Multan, and Karachi, with Matty always as their guide. They had met innumerable prisoners, spoken to every possible person, searching for their relatives who had been seen in PoW camps at the time of war and had never come home. Matty had

79

returned frazzled and silent from the trips. He told her nothing of what he had seen. But he had had nightmares for weeks, thrashing about in his sleep, his breathing harsh and ragged, his teeth clenched (by training, she noted), to prevent any words or cries. At times, he had moaned, a hollow sound full of horrors unknown to her that revisited his mind as he slept. In the mornings, his eyes were bloodshot.

Anita had wanted to ask him what he had seen. But nothing could be said until their drive up to Murree. There, deep amongst the fir trees, outside the embassy-rented bungalow, where bugs couldn't be placed and their shadowers were over a hundred yards, Matty had told her.

"Oh god, that was a risk," she had whispered, shocked and frightened. "What if they find your message? What makes you think they will even let him keep the magazine?"

"It was stupid, I know. But I am sure I met Sharma back in '65. We flew out of his base."

"But you don't even know if it was him . . . and what if we get PNG-ed?" Anita had argued. "Or even whether he will understand what you wrote. He might not even remember. Even I don't remember your call sign from that war. And I am married to you. How could you?"

"I can't tell you why. There are no guarantees anyway, but there is always a chance."

She had simply buried her head in his shoulder, holding him tightly as he stroked her hair.

"Will you mind very much if we get PNG-ed?" he asked after a while. "We can leave our things with the embassy, you know. They will send it all home after us. It isn't like closing down for war." She had laughed against his scratchy green sweater and called him silly.

Standing close together, held by the cold mountain air and scent of pine, they could have been in any of the many cantonment towns they had called home in the first years of their marriage. But as he spoke, Matty had to remind himself that they were both in enemy territory. And Anita was his only companion, his only ally. She needed to know, had a right to know. So he left nothing out, telling her about the stench, the filth, and the pain. About men who lived within the high walls and had retreated into insanity for relief. About prisoners who couldn't believe that he could be from their homeland and wanted proof, even as they dismissed each explanation as an elaborate ruse. About the man his own age, a man with ashen skin stretched taut over what must once have been handsome features, who had collapsed at the sight of Mrs. Sharma and wept dryly into her sari, clutching the cotton in his fists. And finally, about Abu, the tall Pathan.

* * *

Abu was the guard at the Multan jail. He watched implacably from a distance as Matty and the delegation painstakingly went through the lists of foreign prisoners. On the third day, as Matty left the building, he had spoken up: "Janab Captain Sahib, weren't you in the Sialkot sector? With the special ops unit?"

Matty had paused, put his briefcase on the ground next to Abu, who stood guard along the side of the corridor, and crouched to adjust his shoelace. Only for an instant he had hesitated. His cover story, in any case, included a past in the army. "Yes. You were there too?"

"Taken prisoner after battle with the Sikh paltan." Abu had grinned.

"We treated you well, Abu miyan, didn't we?" Matty had said, picking up his briefcase. "Now help us find our men." There had been no time for further words as the jail superintendent accompanying the delegation came up, and Matty had to walk on.

The next day, as he entered the prison gates, he looked for Abu but couldn't find him. In the courtyard where the foreign prisoners had been assembled, he tried to get information about each of them even as the delegation members walked amongst them with time-worn photographs of their loved ones.

"Have you seen this man," they repeated over and over again, holding out black-and-white fragments of memory before unseeing, haunted, terrified eyes. Each time a little flicker of hope would flash through them, slicing through the pain of the years, through the torture of the not-knowing. The hunched figure before them would stare blankly, or sometimes flash a frightened glance at the guards, before shaking his head. "We don't know."

From his rickety desk where he took notes about the prisoners, Matty kept an eye on the delegation, marvelling at their resilience, their determination. He had been concerned about bringing Mrs. Sharma, the only woman amongst the kin, into the prison. Would the prisoners jeer at her, or turn nasty, he had wondered. Instead, her pale, crumpled sari, her soft voice, her gentle demeanour seemed to calm them. No one spoke to her, he noticed, simply shaking their heads as she held out her husband's photograph before them.

She worried him, this woman with her soft voice and sad eyes. *There is no hope*, he wanted to yell at her, shake her by the shoulders. *Look around you, your husband would be better dead than living such horror*, he mentally screamed at her. *There is no hope!* But then he would think of Anita with his photograph in hand, searching, continually searching and ice would grip his insides. It would take all his control to put aside that image and concentrate on the papers before him.

The prisoners would watch continuously as Mrs. Sharma moved around the courtyard. Even when they refused to speak to her, even refused to look at her directly when she spoke to them. Hungrily, furtively, they followed her with their eyes. Once Matty began to wonder what she reminded them of, but then resolutely stopped his mind from going down that particular path. They watched her, pathetic, hungry, sometimes wistful.

That is why no one was prepared for Prisoner Number 351.

* * *

Mrs. Sharma had held back her anguish for days. When the offer to travel with the delegation, to look for Abhayan had been made, it had seemed a beacon of hope. If not Abhayan, then at least she could bring back some news of what had happened to him. All she had was a report from the *Times of India*, dated 12th January, 1972 – a cutting that had been folded and refolded many times, and photocopied again and again – with a list of prisoners of war in Pakistan's jails. Her husband's name was seventeenth on the list.

And, from three years later, a photograph from an American magazine on human rights in jails around the world. Behind the barbed wire, surrounded by starved men in tattered clothing, she was sure, was her husband. The fifth one from the right, pushed up against the barbed wire, his right palm held outward. She had gotten the photograph enlarged and seen what she knew she would. On the inside of his wrist, just under the barbed wire, visible in the enlargement was a small, blue, V-shaped tattoo. V! For her name.

"Now I am branded. Are you quite convinced that I won't be unfaithful?" Abhayan had joked at the Dusshera fair when he had gotten the wizened Gujarati woman to imprint his wife's initial on his skin forever. It had to be the same tattoo, even though the photographer who had enlarged the print had expressed his doubts. "Madam, it could be a printer's smudge . . ."

"In an American magazine?" She had been incredulous. "Do you know how high their standards are? It isn't like our magazines here."

That tattoo had sustained her over the years, always spent hoping for his return.

But the past few days had shaken her. Half-mad men collected in dirty courtyards, wearing nothing but filthy, tattered rags. She had seen their food – dry rotis with some nondescript liquid. Abhayan would hate it here, she thought, with his finicky taste in clothing and his gargantuan appetite for food. She knew that the prisoners shared other details with Captain Mathan (*Mr.* Mathan, she corrected herself. She couldn't give him away). She had heard snatches of conversations, half-sobbed details about beatings and starvation as they spoke haltingly and had steadfastly refused to hear more. Once she caught herself wishing that Abhayan were dead instead of living in such an awful place, but she stopped herself. Just in time.

Then the incident with the prisoner happened. Prisoner Number 351. His right arm placed in a filthy, stained plaster cast, his eyes haunted. She had already showed him Abhayan's picture dozens of times and he had never reacted, not even with a nod. "Please, just see it. His name is Abhayan Sharma. Squadron Leader Abhayan Sharma. Have you seen him?" she had pleaded, holding the photograph before him. "He is my husband. Abhayan Sharma. Have you heard that name?"

He had never responded, staring ahead with unseeing eyes. "Have you heard that name?" she had repeated countless times. They had been told that Prisoner Number 351 was mad, had been so for years. He never spoke to anyone, never cried or moaned. He walked slowly with the other prisoners, day after day, when they were led into the courtyard. And once there, he would settle where he was told and withdraw into some world deep inside himself. Once, on the first day, his eyes had briefly flickered up to Matty. Then he had dropped back into his private, isolated world.

* * *

On the fifth day, Mrs. Sharma had decided not to stop to wave the faded photograph at Prisoner Number 351.

Hesitating slightly, she walked past him, kneeling before the next man, asking her usual, unanswerable question, "Squadron Leader Abhayan Sharma . . . have you seen him? Heard that name?" She never noticed when Prisoner Number 351 pulled himself to his feet, trembling and shuddering as if unaccustomed to the effort. Painfully, slowly, he stumbled towards Mrs. Sharma, who was still kneeling some yards away. With an enormous effort, he lunged towards her, trying to cover the distance with an awkward leap. A strangled, half-wild sound tore free from his throat.

Matty, looking up from his notes only at the sound of the animal moan that broke the silence in the courtyard, sprang to his feet. "Careful, ma'am." At his cry, the guards broke into a run, moving swiftly from their posts by the iron gates that led away from the courtyard. But Prisoner Number 351 had fallen to the ground near Mrs. Sharma, his outstretched hand reaching out to grab an edge of her sari. Harsh moans ripped from his throat, his gnarled fingers clutching at the cotton fabric.

Matty reached the couple first, trying to release the stunned woman from the writhing man. Bending down to pull away the clutched sari, he saw the tears coursing down the grimy cheeks. Stunned by the raw pain in eyes that had held nothing for the past days, he paused.

In that instant, the guards were upon them, struggling to pull the prisoner away, hitting his back and hands with their boots and batons. Putting his arm around Mrs. Sharma's shoulders, Matty tried ineffectually to stop the beatings. "Leave it, chhodo, stop it." Until the ordering tone barked out from his throat: "Stop! Bas!" The guards, instinctively reacting to the authority in his voice, stepped back.

"Are you alright?" Matty asked Mrs. Sharma, self-consciously withdrawing the arm that he had protectively flung around her shoulders.

She nodded, her eyes full of tears. With a visible effort, she tried to steady herself.

Crouching down again, Matty tried to release the folds of her sari that were still clutched in the unbending fingers. Prisoner Number 351 was silent now, the arm with the filthy cast pulled protectively against his chest. But the tears still ran down his cheeks and his eyes were full of an unspoken hunger.

"Please, let go," Matty whispered, moving his fingers firmly over the fist. Prisoner Number 351 wavered for an instant, his eyes devouring the sari-clad figure. Then the fiery eyes grew dim, focussing on a point in the far distance. His shoulders slumped as his fingers uncurled, and he withdrew again into a world of his own.

Matty waited still, searching the grimy, still face before him. "Who are you?" he murmured, but the prisoner had receded far into his inner cell.

"If you don't mind," Mrs. Sharma's voice was soft behind him, "I think I will return to the hotel, Mr. Mathan."

"Yes, of course. Jain here will take you back," Matty spoke hurriedly, pointing towards his assistant from the embassy. "You will understand that I still have to speak to some of them." He couldn't bear to look into her eyes. He had always suspected that sorrow was an infinite well, but the extent of pain in Prisoner Number 351's eyes had shaken him. "You will excuse me, please. I will see you in the evening," he blurted.

"Yes of course, thank you," she murmured, drawing her sari close around her.

* * *

After Mrs. Sharma left, Matty's job was nearly impossible. Prisoner Number 351 had returned to his catatonic state, staring blankly before him, a secret new smile curving around his chapped lips. The other prisoners seemed terrified, or just bewildered, and spoke garbled words, unable to answer the simplest of questions. His frustration mounting, Matty explained again and again, speaking slowly and patiently in Hindi and English, that he would not be returning the next day. Any and all information that the prisoners wished to share with him had to be given that very afternoon. But the inmates were confused, some refusing to speak at all while others rambled wildly or sang tunelessly.

As the evening approached, defeated by the din, Matty began to pack up, putting away his notes. He was about to close his briefcase when he saw the magazine that came from Delhi in the diplomatic bag. Later, when he thought of it, or even tried to explain to Anita, he could find no explanation for what he did next. Quickly, in the guise of making some final notes, he scribbled his phone number on an inner page of the magazine. And instead of his name, he wrote, "Sparrow, 22."

Extracting the magazine, he closed his briefcase with a snap. Walking up to the prisoners lined up against the wall, he found Prisoner Number 351. With a smile, he pushed the magazine, now rolled up, between the plaster-covered hand and the painfully thin chest. "Let him keep it," he told the guards sternly, his officer voice back in place.

"Yes, sir." One of them saluted. Matty walked back to the rickety table and picked up his briefcase with his right hand and gathered the stack of folders he had made on the prisoners in his left.

At the main exit, Abu stood guard. "Salaam aleikum, Captain Sahib," he saluted cheerfully.

"Could you carry these to the car, Abu miyan?" Matty held out the folders. Abu accepted them with alacrity, marching alongside Matty to the embassy car that waited in the parking lot, beyond the barbed wire fence that surrounded the prison.

"Some little help would be good, Abu miyan," Matty muttered. "These men were soldiers, and soldiers should be treated with honour."

Abu nodded in response, smiling widely.

Defeated, Matty reached the car. He turned to receive the folders from Abu and got in. Abu stood aside, waiting to close the door behind him, bending forward slightly.

"Captain Sahib, look for your men in the army prison at Muzaffarabad. Here in Multan, you will not find them. Except on the other side of the jail, and there you can't go. Khuda hafiz, sahib," he murmured.

Matty stared at the tall Pathan looming over the car. Then he smiled as Abu saluted crisply.

Ignoring his orders from home, his training for his present job, and for the first time in two decades since he had given up his uniform, Matty raised his right hand to his forehead in response. "Khuda hafiz, Abu miyan."

* * *

That had been eleven weeks ago. Then the phone call had come, late at night, waking Matty from his nightmares.

"Sparrow 22, Sialkot sector, right?" The voice had been urgent, hoarse.

"Who is this?" Matty had responded, guardedly.

"Squadron Leader Abhayan Sharma. 1963 commission; GD pilot; taken PoW on 4ᵗʰ December, 1971. I am out. Will you help?"

Matty had shot bolt upright at the first words. "Can you get to Islamabad? No, wait, Lahore? Find Hotel Faletti."

"I will try. I will contact you."

"Meet me . . ." Matty began, but the line had gone dead, either cut off by the men who tapped it or because the caller had hung up. With trembling hands, Matty lit a cigarette. He thought of waking Anita, but then how could they talk? Running the shower at three in the morning would be a little ridiculous. No, he would have to wait till the morning.

With a sigh, Matty sank back into the pillows, reaching out under the covers to touch the warmth of his sleeping wife, drawing comfort just from her silent presence next to him. By the time the sun came up the next morning, he had finished his second pack of cigarettes. He had also decided not to inform headquarters about the developments. This one – if it came – would be for Matty alone.

* * *

Days later, on the night of Diwali, as every light in the house blazed, Matty and Anita sat in silence, hand in hand, tense, waiting for the phone to ring again. Hoping to hear from their caller. Before them, alone on the table, a single oil lamp flickered, glowing even amidst the brightness of the electric lights. Glowing in memory of that night, long ago, when a warrior had returned home.

And across the border, slumped in the armchair on her veranda, Mrs. Sharma continued her interminable vigil.

Faded Serge and
Yellowed Lace

She hobbled in every afternoon, just as the bells of the tower at Plaça Rius i Taulet would begin to chime. A little smudge of a woman, frail and old, clad in a long skirt and jumper of nondescript brown and green and beige. I would watch from my balcony as she wound her way slowly to the bench that faced the municipal offices. No one ever sat on that bench, not even the children who played football in the plaza. Once, a wandering tourist sat in her spot, rummaging through his camera case. She stood patiently at a distance until he departed. Then she stumbled over, rushing as if to make up for lost time, and settled in her usual place.

From a ratty old bag of some kind of woven material, she would pull out a piece of cloth, a square patch of something lacy – to spread over her lap. For the next hour, she would glare balefully at the pale facade that enclosed our neighbourhood's bureaucracy, gently stroking the cloth in her lap. Then, as the clock began to strike six, she would carefully fold and put the cloth in her bag, rise painfully and walk away, losing herself in the narrow streets heading down to the Diagonal.

"She's crazy," Marisa from the corner shop told me when I asked her. "Don't believe anything she tells you!" I nodded, as is polite for a foreigner nesting in a foreign city.

"I think her family died in the war," Alex, the American from the bagel shop, explained in a voice that suddenly dropped a few notches. "It's kind of messy, so don't ask."

"No one likes speaking about it. You'll just get people upset," Sergio, the Argentine from the jewellery shop. "It's like our dictatorship. Better not to ask questions."

But as the weeks passed, I noticed that Arturo from the cafe, El Tauro, seemed to know the woman. Every so often, he would take a little something from his kitchen out to her. They never spoke, Arturo and the little old lady. They never even looked at each other.

Instead, Arturo would shuffle over to the bench, seating himself next to her in a furtive manner, almost as if he could will himself invisible. He would slide over a ham and cheese sandwich or a muffin. And just as discreetly, she would nod and cover the offering with a gnarled hand, slide the food into her bag, and never once look away from the building before her. Arturo would sit for a few moments and then sidle back to his cafe.

After a few weeks, I could no longer keep watch and invent stories. "You ask too many questions, maca," Arturo grumbled when I asked him about the old woman. So I bought a carajillo, coffee laced with brandy, and asked him to join me. "You can't bribe me," Arturo sniffed, even as he served the two gut-strippers. "You leave old Carmelita alone, you understand?" he growled at me, jerking his head towards the plaza.

We drank the carajillos in silence, looking out at the laughing children, at couples so in love. "These fancy shops selling expensive things are wrecking the neighbourhood," Arturo complained, pointing to Sergio's shop with its brand-new yellow awnings gleaming in the sun. "Can you believe a silversmith in this place?"

I knew the familiar gripe. The fashionable shops were moving in, driving out the old businesses. Worse still, soon the neighbourhood would cease to be predominantly Catalan and anarchist. "All of history gone in smoke." Even the matter-of-fact Marisa, with her cheeks glowing red, seemed to feel the impending loss.

And through all the changes, there was the old woman's daily vigil. A lone sentinel of the past. At least now I knew her name – Carmelita.

One afternoon, I seated myself next to her on the bench, pretending to read a book, trying to watch her without letting on. Of course, I could have picked up a newspaper but I had learned that newspapers in this country all had connections and memories. People would cut off incipient friendships just because the silly foreigner had erred in buying a newspaper of the wrong affiliation.

Close up, the little napkin she held on her lap seemed a bit tattered. Just three pieces of some faded dark cloth connected by a yellowed net of silk tatting. Much like three fat bugs caught in a spider web. She traced the cloth incessantly, her squat fingertips caressing the three patches over and over again, sliding over the lace threads. And all the while she stared at the pale facade of the municipality with its banners of Spanish and Catalan colours.

On the third day, I slid over a chocolate and raisin biscuit from the Calvet bakery on the Travessera. "Please," I whispered, not sure if I was asking her for a story, or just to take my little offering without offence.

There was a fleeting smile as she raised the brown disc to her nose. "A stranger who likes old things." Her voice was low, so thick that I couldn't be sure if she had spoken at all. "You found the bakery, then." I nodded and smiled as she slipped the biscuit into her voluminous bag without ever looking at me. But I decided I had the permission to watch her, no longer surreptitiously, as her fingers moved on her lap and her eyes remained fixed before her.

"Her family was killed in the war," Arturo informed me when I walked into the cafe for my coffee. "Have a carajillo instead. It will do both of us good." He brought the two steaming cups over to the end of the ragged linoleum bar. He hid behind his cup, frowning. "For so many years, no one asks. And then we get you . . . a foreigner, harassing poor old people like us." I grinned in what I thought was a sympathetic manner.

After a few days, having watched me sit with Carmelita, he seemed to have made up his mind. "Her father and two brothers were killed. The police or the soldiers . . . who knows who did it. A lot of people were taken away when the war ended." He finally muttered, sighing as if the words had been wrung from him. "Manolo was the youngest. We were friends."

"So, what happened?" I persisted, feeling at once like a child begging for a story and an uninvited guest at a funeral.

"There were fusilamientos, people shot. Buried quietly in the night, somewhere no one knew." Arturo spoke into the empty cup, his mouth barely moving, his face scrunched into a frown. I waited, silent, patient, feeling increasingly like a vulture.

"They needed people to move the bodies. It was not work for soldiers. No dirty hands for them. That was for people who worked in the night, moving, loading the dead into trucks. Getting the smell of blood on our hands." I sat still, barely daring to breathe.

"We tore bits off the clothes to bring back. Sometimes, people recognised who had been shot. From the scraps." His voice seemed to rise from some long-forgotten prison inside. Strangled. Harsh. Barely audible. "Ya basta." Arturo shook himself, "we need some brandy. My invitation." He turned away, blindly moving the bottles on the shelf, the memories pushed back into their jail cell and locked away.

Something shifted after hearing Arturo's story. Carmelita's daily vigil seemed to grow sinister. For a day or two afterwards, I could not bring myself to go down into the plaza to sit with her. Instead, I hid behind the bougainvillea on my balcony and watched as Arturo took coffee to Carmelita. She didn't touch the cup that he left on the bench next to her. And after she walked away, Arturo returned again and poured the cold remains onto the roots of a straggly tree.

Three days later, I felt as if I were being drawn by an invisible thread. Tense and upset, I made my way downstairs to sit on the bench. Carmelita had not yet arrived. A few minutes still remained till the clock would strike five. Behind the glass front of El Tauro, Arturo seemed to be standing guard, his white shirt glowing against the gloom of the cafe.

As the bells began tolling, Carmelita walked up. "Bona tarda," she murmured politely as she seated herself next to me. Minutes ticked by as she began the ritual – pulling out the cloth and spreading it carefully on her lap. Her eyes rose to rest on the facade before us. Her fingers gently began tracing their familiar path over the material. I sat still, staring ahead, not daring to look at her.

"See this," she commanded, startling me. I turned to look at her. Her rough hand had grasped my wrist. She pulled it over her lap, pushing my fingers down onto the cloth. I looked down, watching as her blue-veined, liver-spotted hand dragged mine over the cloth. A small square patch that might once have been blue. A rectangle, slightly bigger, of some grey cloth. A brown triangle with what appeared to be a red stripe through it. Faded pieces of serge bleeding into a yellow spider web. An incongruous sight of bits of old cloth linked together by twelve-petalled lace flowers.

"The number of petals mark the skill of the lace-maker," I remembered hearing somewhere. Perhaps in the market. Or from Marisa.

She dragged my fingers on the cloth. I would have snatched them back, as if from a hot stove, but her grip was strong, insistent. I had asked for a story. Instead, I would get a tour of an intimate cemetery, a look at a memorial as ghastly as blue numbers on ageing pale skins.

"My father . . ." The grey patch.

"Tono . . ." The faded blue.

"Manolo." A sob seemed to die within her throat as my fingers touched the triangle.

They moved slowly over the cloth, dragged by Carmelita. The faded serge, smooth like polished marble. The silk of the lace, like so many deep crevices that could swallow up worlds. And a rage like molten lava bubbling under a volcano with such a force that one could only pray it never found its way out.

Suddenly, she let go of my hand, letting me snatch it back. I sucked on my fingertips, part for some childish comfort, part as if they had been scorched. Carmelita gathered up her cloth and rose to leave. I looked up at her and she seemed to smile, her dull cataract-lined eyes lighting up with sudden fierceness. She patted my shoulder.

"They didn't get all of us, hija. They won't get me."

In the Vauxhall Pleasure Gardens

Graham has always been wary of honey traps. After all, he's spent nearly four decades paying for them. They always show up the same way, even now, starting with some extra receipts for drinks, in nice pubs. In fashionable cocktail lounges and low-key, offbeat bars. Then over time, there are gaps in spending, or an odd receipt for a night or two in a cosy, picturesque, out-of-the-way inn. Finally, and he knows this is when things go very wrong, there are the unexplainable, unexplained holes in operational funds.

The guys in the field think they are being discreet, will never be caught, but Graham learned early on to identify the signs. Simply because he must ensure he isn't paying too much for similar activities by his own operatives.

Although that's stretching the truth – it is Her Majesty who really pays – his job has long been to make sure that her money is appropriately spent. He looks carefully through all the receipts, from Budapest, Baghdad, even Bogotá on one occasion, though he tries to forget that that operation had gone particularly poorly. He knows the exchange rates, and prices for drinks, meals, and coffees in cities around the world. His eyes are sharp for any treats that the boys in the field may want to slip through.

At the beginning, when they were still in the old offices, he had checked against the guidebooks in the office library, laboriously estimating price rises against economic indices. Now it just takes a few clicks on his computer. Not that he even needs to do that any more, he has a whole team these days, albeit one that's constantly being depleted by the ongoing budgetary cuts to monitor Her Majesty's expenses. Still, one likes to stay in form and keep an eye on the young ones, who seem to grow more feckless with each new intake.

When he was younger, he sometimes would wonder about far off places: Moscow, Delhi, Kampala. Not that he had any desire to go to them. He always took his three weeks of annual leave on the Cornish coast, just as he had as a boy. But perhaps he would need to change that now. The old lady who managed the cottage had died just the year before, and he didn't think her flighty daughter would quite manage to keep things just so. And soon, he'd have more time than the annual three weeks. Graham tried not to think of the change that loomed not so far ahead.

As a born-and-bred Londoner, he was at home in the city that the world clamoured to make its own. Or perhaps he was just a creature of habit, like the suits that he always bought in the same colour every second year during January sales from Marks & Spencer's. He waved that thought away. No one who lived in a shape-shifting city like his could ever be a creature of habit. Even less so given his professional affiliation. So, he liked things to be calm, ordered. Just as he liked the daily brisk walk across the bridge from his bachelor flat in Pimlico, down Albert Embankment to the new building, and then up to his office. He had preferred the old offices, a bit rundown and grey, and draughty. They fitted him better, like his painstakingly polished but battered old brogues, each scuff and fold of the leather a sign of history, of character – as his grandfather had often said.

The new building seemed hollow, its shining facade a proclamation of the power that all knew had ebbed away. In a secret, never-to-be-spoken-of part of his mind, Graham thought of it as a folly. Worse still, all these years later, he had still not grown accustomed to crossing the river each day, to the daily trips south. His few prejudices ran deep, though he refused to consider them thus. It was just the healthy disdain of a decent man for the decrepit remains of the Pleasure Gardens. In the early days of the move, he deliberately did not look across the street to where shabby, colourful denizens congregated under the dark arches. Walking briskly, his nose would curl unconsciously, imperceptibly, at the faint scent of mildew he was sure hung over the neighbourhood. Occasionally, he feared that they were much like the people he paid to do Her Majesty's work, but he quickly pushed away that treasonous thought.

For quite some time, Graham avoided crossing under the railway. He pretended that nothing existed beyond and returned across the river for his after-dinner pint before heading home. Of course, he varied his routine, and his routes, as the training manuals instructed. But then slowly, imperceptibly, as the surroundings gentrified, the Vauxhall pretty boys vanished from the shadows and shiny new builds replaced the shabby old streets, he began to settle in.

Graham's walk across the river and down the Embankment is still brisk, intended to get his heart pumping a bit better. He has even grown accustomed to looking out the window and at the city from an upside-down perspective, remembering only occasionally to note how it looks quite different from the south, and across the water. If he still feels a sudden occasional panic at being outside the city, gazing at it from afar, that is only normal for someone who had never crossed south of the Thames till his eighteenth birthday.

He discovered the Black Dog a few years after the move to the new offices. None of the others from his section liked it much, finding little of interest or comfort in the shabby pub. After work, he began to cross under the tracks, and then to the small garden. He always sat on the bench for a bit, working on the crossword puzzle in his daily paper, always facing the tea house. The tea house has changed as well in the past couple of years. It is a theatre *and* tea house now, and antiseptically pristine. The pretty boys, the prostitutes, the peddlers are all gone. Graham wonders occasionally if he misses them, but is quite sure he doesn't. There is more pleasure now in the shabby gardens than there had been before. The benches are clean, and he likes hearing the young men play on the caged basketball court as he painstakingly completes his crossword. Before things were cleaned up, people would stop to ask him for cigarettes, or money, but not any more. Yes, he prefers the Pleasure Gardens of now. There is a sense of purpose to the people walking straight through, to the theatre-cafe, the pub, or the basketball court. No lingering or malingering, he tells himself, repeating a phrase from his childhood.

He finishes his crossword and pops into the Black Dog for his usual pint, always taking it to the little table in the corner, nearest the door to the beer garden, almost invisible from the glass windows and prying eyes. There's something comforting about the old-fashioned wallpaper and vintage sconces. The silent Bakelite radio reminds him of his mum's stories. They used to have one at home when he was growing up but it had disappeared somewhere once he left home. Just the one pint, each time, and then the walk back across the river. It's a comforting routine, and increasingly, in the moments when his thoughts stray, he recognises that he'll miss it. But not till the year after, not till retirement, or "freedom" as some in the office call it.

* * *

Graham saw her on an early day of spring, though of course he'd seen her before. Weeks before, noting her presence as only a slight disturbance that first time. Or rather the second week. Casuals came through the park regularly. He'd learned to clock and discard them instantly. But he noticed her that first day, and then through the week. She looked like a woman who could have been beautiful once, if she had tried. Her features were even, and there was dignity in her bearing, in the measured steps, in the squaring of her shoulders as she stopped to choose a bench. He noted that she deliberately turned her eyes away from the train line and the shiny glass monster beyond as if she found them unseemly. Then as she settled in to read on the bench next to him, he noticed that her fingers were long, graceful, with unpainted, clean short nails. And around the book she held, her hands were steady. She hadn't gone into the pub afterwards and had instead walked off down the street, heading south.

He'd expected her to be gone after the weekend, like all those staying at the affordable business hotels that edged the gardens, and had felt a sudden frisson when she appeared on the following drab Monday. And again, on the days that followed. They never spoke beyond the initial greeting, though he thought he could recognise her voice anywhere. Soft with flat vowels, something that could have been an accent, but unrecognisable. Or at least, he would know her voice if she said, "Good afternoon." But he'd grown accustomed to their half hour of silent companionship, seated side by side on the bench, his crossword, her books. He never quite caught the titles that she read, but had sneaked enough glances to know that she preferred old editions with dark hardcovers and brittle cream pages.

He wasn't sure when he began looking for her, when he first felt a nervous flutter as he settled himself on the bench and wondered if she'd come. But he remembers that first moment as he ironed his shirts for the week ahead, watching the news on a Sunday night, when he had found himself smiling. Monday. He'd see her the next afternoon. An unfathomable wave of sudden terror had swept over him and his stomach had hollowed. What if she didn't come? He'd shaken himself angrily, telling himself off for being an old fool. But as the man on the telly droned on about bombs in one of the places he knew only from the office receipts, he'd found himself wondering what her grey hair would feel like through his fingers. She wore it up, in one of those severe twists at the back of her head. He had seen it catch the afternoon light and knew it would feel soft, full, in his hands. Just like the rest of her.

He learned her name one afternoon when she answered a phone call. Graham had been a bit annoyed at the intrusion of sounds, but she was brief, with many yeses, noes, and of courses, walking away a little from the bench for privacy. But he had noted the first sentence she had spoken. "This is Catherine." He liked the sound of the name, turning it over in his mind, relieved at its stability, yet vaguely disappointed that it was so commonplace.

"I'm so sorry." Her voice was low when she returned to her place on the bench, her lips twisting wryly. "Family." He had smiled and nodded, too shocked to respond with more. But later he remembered that her eyes were warm, with tiny laugh lines at the creases.

* * *

Spring turned to summer, and Graham lingered longer over his crossword. They seemed to grow harder to solve in the warmth of the sunshine, though he knew it was more because he couldn't stop watching Catherine from the corner of his eye. He wondered if all her skin was as soft as it seemed on her forearms. She shed her winter coat for a mac and he found himself wanting to span her belted waist with his hands. He thought he knew her scent now, musky with something floral and clean, but that may have been his mind playing tricks. But they were the kinds of tricks he wanted more of each day.

They say goodbye now, Catherine and Graham, though he has never told her his name. He finishes his crossword, taking a bit longer each day, folds his paper, and stares ahead at the young people crowding the theatre-cafe. In the summer light, he can almost feel the heat from her. Sometimes, when he lets his eyes stray a little, he knows the distance between them grows imperceptibly smaller, the glossy dark span of wood between her beige mac and his grey suit just a little narrower each day. But then perhaps this is a trick his mind plays as well. Catherine now reads for a little longer, just a couple of minutes, then marks the page in her book and puts it away and they sit there for a bit. She is always first to rise off the bench, and waits for him. "See you tomorrow," four times a week. And then "See you next week," on Fridays. Her teeth are small, very even, and her smile warms him up from the inside. They walk side by side for a few steps, almost like friends or lovers, to the edge of the Pleasure Gardens, till she turns south into Laud Street, and he steps into the shadows of the Black Dog.

Some nights, alone in his flat, Graham wonders what it would be like to speak to her further. Perhaps he should ask her to join him for a drink. Or perhaps tea. Perhaps they would come back to his flat. Or go to hers? Would she be soft all over? But that near-inaudible hint of an accent makes him wary, though he tells himself times have changed. This is London, his boss had said some days ago, everyone has an accent now. But old habits are too deeply rooted and he has seen too many good men falter to take such a chance. Sometimes he wonders if he should ask one of the others to run a check on her. It should be easy enough with all the money they have put into databases over the years. But the thought of sharing her with anyone, even, *especially*, at work, fills him with horror. Even worse is the thought of empty afternoons, of nothing but his crossword, of sitting alone on their bench again.

This is also why Graham has been increasingly anxious this afternoon. He is to go away on Monday for his holiday and is too afraid to even wonder if she'll miss him. Yet he has caught himself worrying that she won't think of him or that she'll find other company for her evenings. Or, worst of all, that she will no longer come to the park when he returns. That she will disappear forever.

He plans to ask her for a number or an address. He has always wanted to send someone those postcards they sell in the village off-licence.

As he crosses the Albert Embankment, then strolls under the train tracks and through the tunnel, he feels a sudden surge of excitement, as he always does these days. The essence of the Pleasure Gardens, even though little remains of all that was once glorious and louche. She is there first today, seated already on their bench. As he walks along the winding path, he can feel his stomach knot. Her arms are bare today, he notices, with a sudden lurch. A summer dress that makes her seem younger, lighter, than he has ever imagined. As he nears, he sees she has placed her mac next to her, almost as if to reserve his spot.

Her eyes are warm, her smile wide as she looks up from the book, moving her mac to her lap to make room for him. "Good afternoon."

Graham can feel his heart thump. Even to his own ears, his voice sounds like a croak. He can think of nothing to say as he pulls out his crossword. Her arms look as soft as he has imagined. Under her dress, he can see the shape of her thighs. He wants to run his fingers over the skin he knows will be softer still, fill his palm with the curve of her. They stay longer than ever before, almost till the park starts to empty and dinner tables fill up. He hasn't finished his crossword and she keeps reading, the edge of her mac almost flush against his thigh.

"We won't see each other any more. Not after today." When she finally speaks, her voice is low, soft, almost a question.

"Yes, not for three weeks."

'Graham, you must know.' She has turned to him. He can smell her now. Something floral and musky and expensive. His eyes catch at the hollow of her throat, where a web of fine lines criss-crosses her skin. He wants to lean in and run his tongue against it. His breath catches as her lips seem to draw closer. Then he feels her hand move, light against his thigh. Warm, gentle. Then something fleeting and sharp.

"How do you know my name?" he wants to ask, but her scent fills his nose. Her lips are moist, slightly parted. A bit blurred, perhaps because they fill his eyes so completely.

"This is just a message. Nothing personal." Her breath is warm against his cheek. Graham wants to move, to lift his hands to pull her close. To draw her in for a kiss, but his body has frozen. No words push past his tongue. She reaches up to pull the clip from her hair, freeing it. Streaks of grey flood past her shoulders, a tendril reaching out towards his face.

"But this is. This is personal." Her lips touch his, gently, quickly, just once. As soft as he had imagined. Then she is moving away, her mac in her arms, turning left on the path and then south. He watches her leave, his vision blurring as she recedes into the distance, his head growing ever heavier, and his breaths increasingly slower and harsher. As he slumps on the bench, he thinks she turns around and smiles.

Tulips

Lyndsey always buys flowers for herself.

Since coming home, she buys them regularly, at times paying exorbitant prices, and is grateful for Sally-Mae who stocks them all year round. She likes to have twenty-seven in the vase, the perfect number, the true number, but feels a little awkward when she asks for three extras to round up the two dozen.

Once when she bought them from the shop in the mall, they only sold them by the dozen. She had stood at the garbage can near the food court picking out nine extra stems. A trickle of sweat had traced down her back as she pulled them out to toss them in the trash. She had clenched her jaw so hard it had been sore for days afterwards. She plans ahead now, checking availabilities with Sally-Mae when the flowers begin to wither even though she waits as the petals droop and contort and darken, until they drop softly to the counter. She prefers the darker ones – violets and reds, and sometimes oranges bleeding into maroons, or pinks turning into purples. And she likes them better when they begin to wilt, the delicate petals spreading outward, reaching downward, bruising into mottled brown and black.

Once the curling petals begin to fall off, she gets ready to replace them, following a familiar, soothing ritual. Now she only buys them from Sally-Mae, even though the pretty flower shop makes her feel ugly, takes her back to school when the popular girls didn't like her, when the boys ignored her. Most of the time, Lyndsey is sure that she can see a faint disdainful wrinkle in Sally-Mae's nose before her bright laughter takes over.

Sally-Mae never asks her probing questions, which is a relief. She also keeps Lyndsey's flowers wrapped and ready. "You been ok?" she asks every time, almost as if they are friends. Once, when another customer had grumbled about the slow service, Sally-Mae had waved her shiny florist scissors and sternly announced, "This lady here served three tours in those damn sandpits to keep us safe. We can all wait till she's served." Lyndsey had flushed in embarrassment and mumbled thank you and sorry before rushing away.

"Thank you for your service," Sally-Mae says each time, and adds a veteran's discount before placing bright, unbruised tulips in Lyndsey's arms. She seems sincere but Lyndsey wonders if she truly means those words, worries that she's found out about the dishonourable discharge. Mostly she wonders if she's being thanked for the same services for which she's been tried, sentenced, shamed. She holds her blooms tenderly, close to her heart, on her way home.

* * *

In court, her lawyers had argued that Lyndsey had been coerced: by her superior officer, by Big Pete, and by others in her unit. They insisted that she had acted under duress. She had gone along with it, though she knew better. She never tells anyone that she volunteered. Not that she'd done it out loud, of course. Lyndsey learned early on that it is better to offer to do things without words, without leaving any trace, to promise without ever saying anything at all.

One of the officers called it plausible deniability when they were preparing her for the trial. She wishes she had known that term when her first date pushed her head down on his cock. He wasn't even on the football team, just a hanger-on, but he had asked her out, even paid for their beers. In the backseat of his Cherokee, she had held her neck stiff, even whimpered quietly, at the start. His fist had clenched in her hair, hurting just a bit, and he had pushed her down harder till she had opened her lips and taken him in. No promises, no threats, no traces, no evidence. Plausible deniability. That's how she knew that her lover had not coerced her.

Big Pete had held her close instead, his eyes lighting with desire, when he saw her swish her hips as she walked past the cages. He laughed out loud as the men behind bars lowered their eyes. His cock had grown hard faster than ever before when she had first told him she wanted to try a dog leash on those men. "How about making them crawl to enhanced interrogation?" she had murmured in his ear as he had pushed into her over and over again.

He would be back soon from Afghanistan, Iraq, wherever he was these days. He still writes to her, although without plans whispered in bed, without his sweat-soaked skin above hers, his words are dull. The brass have clamped down on what can be put in emails and messages: "Yeah, we do it, but don't fucking write home about it. And not to the damn civilians." She feels a flash of anger. She shouldn't be a civilian, not for doing what they all knew was right, for what they all did at the Facility then, are still doing somewhere else now.

* * *

Lyndsey hadn't known about tulips as a child. They didn't grow anywhere she knew. She remembers a classmate bringing in pictures for a history project. Of cities with narrow canals, windmills like hulking beasts and happy, golden people. She hadn't paid much attention until a postcard of a bright field full of red, yellow, pink-blue, all laid out in precise rows, like soldiers at a parade. At lunch, she'd traded two weeks' allowance and three weeks' homework for that postcard. She had pinned it over her bed, where it would be the first and last thing she saw each day, so she could lie staring at the colours, whispering their name like a prayer – tulips, toolips, tyulips, tulips – and wishing she could be where they grew. Even when she learned that those were actually hyacinths, a word too ugly for the flowers she had loved at first sight, the postcard remained precious, and she whispered the word each night until she could make herself believe.

The postcard was faded and dog-eared by the time she first saw real tulips, in a real painting. Reds, yellows, pinks, purples. Not like soldiers at all. One colour bleeding into another until her eyes ached from just looking. She could have stayed all day, all her life, staring at that field of tulips, but her class was hurried along too soon. As the teacher rushed them off to another room of the museum, she had turned back for a final look. From a distance, the heads were no longer distinct. Instead, the colours had blurred into a single, enormous bruise, held tight by the ornate gilt frame. Lyndsey had promised herself that she would seek them out as soon as she was able.

Perhaps that's why she went looking for the flowers while her unit waited at a base before flying farther east. By then she'd already seen more postcards, photos in guidebooks, even pictures of other paintings. The commissary sold wooden ones for the folks heading home, the bulbous heads – reds, yellows, pinks – balanced on rigid stalks. After waiting for so long to see them in real life, she had expected to be disappointed, had told herself that nothing else had ever matched her expectations, so why should they?

Yet when she first spotted them, she was transfixed. As if they had been waiting for her.

In a flower shop in the centre of town, placed carefully in a tall glass vase. The pale green stems sprouted straight up. The heavy dark heads snuggled against the sharp rim. "They're too heavy to be held up on those stems," the florist had explained, her accent not unpleasant. Lyndsey had lingered, inhaling the sickly sweet odour of the shop till the florist gave her a conspiratorial smile and unboxed a fresh bunch to lay out on the counter. "There is another way. And nobody is ever the wiser, except those of us who know."

Lyndsey waited, holding her breath.

"You must make them stand up straight," the florist murmured as if talking to herself, her pale blue eyes focussed entirely on the head held between her fingers. She gave a little hum, cradling it against her palm, steadying it with her thumb and ring finger as she plunged the tip of a sharp, ornate instrument carefully into the base of the bud.

"Some use needles, but I think an awl has more control." Just below the petals, at the base, where the stalk began. The silver spike disappeared into the core, but as Lyndsey shifted, she could see the tip shine on the other side, against the florist's pink palm. The glow of the old lamp on the counter caught the knot of the florist's hair, glistening on the blonde strands, drowning in the dull grey. It twinkled on the rings on her hands, and on the antique silver sewing awl which she drove so precisely into each unopened flower. Lyndsey's unease must have shown on her face as the woman carefully stabbed again, then again, into the tulips. Perhaps that is why she paused to smile.

"Don't worry, it's all for the good. They last for days like this."

* * *

From the very beginning, Lyndsey liked the power of walking naked into the interrogation room. The cells were air-conditioned and they liked keeping the air-con running on high. The cold reminded her of home, let her pretend that it wasn't filthy and disgusting beyond the perimeter. And the cold was worse for the prisoners, naked, spread against the industrial white tiles, the metal shackles freezing against their ankles and wrists. But most of all she liked the fear and humiliation in their eyes as they looked at her goose-bumped skin, her stiff nipples, her taut abs, her shaven pussy. She had never felt anything like that before coming out to this hell hole of dust and gunpowder and heat and sweat. But here, striding down the narrow corridors between the cells, the air-con turned high, and her hips swishing just a bit, here she knew what it was like for the girls from the Heights back home. Why they are always sexy, and strong, and in control, and *pretty*.

Back home, most guys look past her, barely noticing her snub nose, field mouse hair, small breasts. Until they are drunk, and it is the end of the night. Or when they are old, and gross, and she wants to hide from the revulsion they provoke in her. For years she had thought those were the only ways men would, could, look at her. With reluctant lust. And bleary contempt. And the morning after, if there was one, with bored disdain.

But that was before she was deployed to the Facility. High security of course, which meant a real nice extra bit on her pay check. Plus, there was the hardship pay which she squirrelled away, not that there was much to spend it on except booze and pills and sometimes a cut to the medic, who ran a sideline getting rid of complications. "Hey, don't stress. We don't beat ours out of the womb," he had grinned the first time she worried about a broken condom.

"Keeping that one for the locals, eh?"

"Yeah, and other tricks you should be grateful you'll never find out," he had winked. His name was Simon and for a long time she had thought he liked her and not only because he liked to make her come, not even because he liked to cuddle after fucking her. Till he testified at the trial. Against her. That piece of shit! At least Big Pete really seemed to like her even though he always fucked her mouth till she couldn't breathe.

Still, the Facility was far from the war, even from the nutters who regularly tried to run the near-impassable concrete barriers in rickety vehicles stuffed with IEDs. The quarters were also air-conditioned, cool despite the fiery heat that rippled against the triple-glazed windows. And the commissary had everything you could want, like they'd never left stateside at all. Lyndsey knew it was a good deal, a better deal than she'd ever hoped for, especially since the first two tours had been shit.

Soon after her arrival she'd noticed how the detainees looked at her. With anger. And fear. With despair, and at times, if they were very young, with a shred of hope. But mostly with shame, though she never understood for whom. Her? For themselves? In their furtive, agonised eyes, she discovered power of a kind that she had never imagined, a rush more potent than any drug she'd taken, a pleasure greater than any she'd found before.

Which is why when Big Pete asked her to question the first one, she'd said yes. He'd watched her, told her how to rub herself, to run her hands over that terrorist fucker who yanked on his restraints and shouted into the gag. And he had laughed when tears leaked out of those aged, humiliated eyes. She'd winked and grinned, writhing like a stripper against the slumped body, feeling hot like a girl in a music video. And when Big Pete had fucked her afterwards, she had come like never before in her life.

* * *

Her family isn't the sort to have flowers around, so Lyndsey's father had laughed at her the first time she brought home some of the pretty ones that grew along the path back from school. "Why'd you bring weeds?" He didn't seem angry so she had mumbled something he would have thought was an apology, and taken the little bunch to the kitchen to put them in a tumbler full of water. "We don't live in the Heights, girl," he had told her later, when he'd had a few beers. She didn't bring home any more weeds, but she started to pay attention. The popular girls, she learned, smell like flowers, instead of soap and sweat.

One afternoon, she had pedalled up the slope to the big houses with green lawns and flowers in neat beds. She knew there were pools in the back because she had heard her classmates talk of parties. Her eyes had prickled with something she has never felt before: a blinding fury. At not being invited. At her dull field mouse hair that flops about her ears. At her too-short legs, at her clothes that don't fit right; at her mother, who works at the mall and smells of Lysol instead of sweet flowers, and at her own house, with its faded paint and overgrown yard.

Her heart had pounded, her head had felt like it was on fire. Her eyes had stung, and her ears had felt like she was suddenly underwater. She had lost her balance, and the bike had toppled over onto the softest, greenest grass she'd ever felt. Instantly, an alarm began to shriek. She ignored the deafening squeal and sat up, dragging herself and her bicycle back to the concrete of the sidewalk.

A woman had appeared at the window beyond the lawn, her arms full of flowers, her hair glossy even behind the glass. Her face was small and pink, pinched in annoyed enquiry. Lyndsey had grinned in what she hoped was a polite way and waved her arms about in a frantic, silent apology. The woman had given a single nod – like a queen, Lyndsey thought – and turned away, her hair following behind her.

In that instant, Lyndsey knew. She wants to be that woman in the window, with an armful of sweet-smelling flowers, with swishy hair and a little pink face, in a big house with a green, soft lawn.

The alarm had fallen silent when she started to push her bike back down the slope.

* * *

Since he's moved to town, Simon has pretended that he doesn't know her. She bets he was dishonourably discharged as well. He works at the hospital just across from the cafe where she has a few shifts. He had come in once, while she was at the till, and turned first pale, then so red as to be nearly purple. Lyndsey is impressed that he can still manage that sharp about-turn, especially when running out the door. She hasn't seen him in the cafe since, though he often strides past the window, refusing even to glance her way.

A few months ago, she realised that they go to the same church, although Simon doesn't come to service regularly. She likes to think he's ashamed of what he's done. Testifying against her as if he was some kind of pinko, treating enemies like friends. As if he hadn't fucked her and then cuddled her and taught her how to inflict pain without leaving a trace.

"You tell me if it works, and I'll make you come just with my mouth." He's the only man she's met who likes doing that, so she does. And he does, after he's listened to her explain.

"Give me more details," he had demanded each time, his eyes bright, his lips shiny, as if her words alone could make him drool. Of course, the fucker didn't talk about that at the trial. He didn't even correctly tally up her count: twenty-seven. That's how many she broke to keep everyone safe. Not a word of that. Instead, he testified about three instances. Instances! As if she hadn't done everything he'd taught her. Three. Only three! She only learned then that he hadn't signed off on the others, that those files had other names and signatures. Lyndsey thinks he's ashamed. She hopes he's ashamed. As he should be, for his lies. For acting like they didn't do everything they could to keep folk back home safe. Mostly she rages that his lies make her sound like a lost little girl. Plausible deniability, the officers had said. Coercion, her lawyers had argued. She'd gone along with it, but she hates feeling powerless again.

When she hears at church that Simon is dead, she stays to listen. He walked off the rooftop of the hospital, someone says. PTSD, someone else whispers. Things he saw and experienced over there. She imagines Simon, with his glistening smile and wide eyes, his soft voice that hides the delight he takes in finding new, secret ways of inflicting pain. If she closes her eyes, she can see his childlike wonder at discovering that his book-learning works. Why did Simon, with his talented tongue that buys him time and attention, even affection from women, throw himself off a roof? She reminds herself that she doesn't really care about Simon, even though she liked him better than the men who fucked her but forgot about her pleasure. Simon lied about her, testified against her, teased her, pleased her, cuddled her. Ignored her. Pretended that she had stopped existing.

Simon had told her that knowing things was the secret to power. Lyndsey feels a sudden fury. She knows. She thought Simon had known, too. Hadn't he taught her? How could it be PTSD? They didn't even go into battle, and the Facility was their kingdom. Nobody hurt them. Nobody could. She wants to shake him, slap him, pull his face into her cunt till he remembers, until she cares.

Simon, with his wide eyes and slick mouth, walking off the hospital roof. She can see him plunging through the air, landing with a thud. On the sidewalk? Or the loading bay? The parking lot? Then the anger fades. She's glad he's dead. Simon with his lies, his testimony, his pretence, his refusal to give her the kills she made. She's glad he's dead.

* * *

At first, she hadn't known how to do it right. A hesitant jab, a too-thick needle, too much force, everything conspired against her. Just weeks after her discharge – fuck the dishonourable – the money had appeared in her account. Sometimes she thought of it as hush money, but then remembered that she had stayed silent.

Soon after, Big Pete emailed her, his words dull and predictable with promises of returning stateside, full of fantasies of sex and things they could do together that had her snort in disbelief, disgust, contempt. They had done nothing but fuck together and sometimes she wasn't even sure if that counted.

The day Simon walked into the cafe she had picked up a bunch, only six, on her way home. But her fingers fumbled and trembled, and she had ruined two red blooms. Frustrated, she had slammed the rest into a jug of water but when they began drooping within hours, she had grabbed them to crush them in her clenched fists. Standing over the sink, she had shredded the petals, ripped the leaves and finally cut up the stems with a knife.

The next time Sally-Mae thanked her for her service, she had mumbled a request, telling her of the florist with the antique silver awl, blurting out half-sentences and muddled words. Sally-Mae hadn't laughed, instead told her to return at closing time. Then she'd taught Lyndsey the real trick, known only to a few.

Now she knows to first hold the stems under a thin stream of water, to snip a half-inch off the stem with a clean, sharp knife. Lyndsey finds it soothing, almost meditative, to lay them out in a row, evenly spaced on a white linen cloth on the grey kitchen counter. She measures out just the right amount of water into the vase and drops in three ice cubes.

Usually, she takes time to examine them as they lie still, runs her fingertip slowly up the stems, barely brushing the heavy heads. Lined up on the white linen, they look like corpses. Then gently picking a bud, she prepares herself.

She cups the fragile bloom in her palm, gathers herself with a deep breath. She ignores Sally-Mae's advice and instead steadies it with her thumb and ring finger, just like the florist in that faraway city with canals. It's always the same: a quick, sharp jab with a darning needle to the base of the head. Just above the slender stem. A clean push to stab past the resistant flesh. Then a slow, gentle pull back.

Today, she thinks of Simon. And of how she'd walk the detainees into their cells afterwards. Of the way they would stand stiffly, eyes vacant, the occasional bruise rising where some newbie had slipped up. She'd start walking away, counting the seconds, anxious to work off the adrenalin rushing through her. By the sixth step, there would be a soft exhale, just loud enough to make her turn. Then the head would droop, the body would slowly – ever so slowly – fold into itself, like a balloon losing air, until it sank to the floor. Finally, there would be that unmistakable thud of flesh hitting the cold tile. Lyndsey wonders if Simon sounded like that when he stepped off the roof of the hospital. In the loading bay. Thud. In the parking lot. Thud. On the sidewalk. Thud.

She replaces the punctured stalk on the expanse of white, the linen folds cradling the bloom like a shroud.

She remembers the satisfaction of fucking Pete. Of cleaning up to race to Simon to tell him that his teaching had worked, again.

Before her, the tulips lie in a clean row – red, pink, purple. Like dead men. Like dead men who died in immense pain, with injuries that nobody saw. Of invisible wounds that bled until they wilted and fell. She runs a gentle finger along the heads lined up before her. And breathes deep once more. Slowly, methodically, deliberately, she picks up the next one. And the next. Until she reaches the end of the line. Until she lays the last one back down and gently ruches up the linen around them.

She counts them again, in a whisper, as she places each one against the sharp glass edge of the vase. One . . . four . . . thirteen . . . nineteen . . . twenty-four . . . And when the space is seemingly full, unable to take any more, Lyndsey makes room for three more, prodding gently till they all fit.

Twenty-seven. The number of the dead men at the Facility. Twenty-seven, like the files on Simon's desk. Like her true kill number.

Not My Mountains

More than anything else, it's the cold that makes Edgar "Eddie" Ao decide that these mountains shall never be his. Before the unit moved up from the plains, they said this was paradise on earth but he thinks they lied.

As he stands on sentry duty yet another night, he misses the gentle chill of home that can sneak past a loosened collar and slip down the spine, shocking yet delightful, full of laughter, like one of his brother's pranks. The cold here is dry, and so brutal that it hurts to draw in a breath, as if the frozen air itself were the enemy. He squints into the night, the dark beyond the high-powered lights so deep, so empty, that he can only imagine the bare rocky crags in the distance. They are nothing like the clinging mists of his hills and valleys, nothing like the green-covered hills that bloom with a thousand plants all year round.

Here, the cold is so terrible that simply standing still too long can kill a man. The havildar has grown old in the regiment, but even he finds these mountains terrifying. He shouts at them to keep moving even in the sentry box, warns them that here a man can grow so cold that merely stretching his arms can crack a rib, or more. Three of the men in their platoon have already been sent down to the valley hospital in the past two weeks and Havildar Sahab says the winter is just setting in.

Everything freezes in these mountains, he thinks. Just yesterday, when his section had been on patrol, somebody had cracked a joke. It was so bad that Eddie does not remember it. But they had all laughed, laughed so hard that they had cried. Then the tears had frozen on their cheeks and that had hurt. He knows about the air sticking in his throat like grit or cold cement, burning a trail up his nose and all the way into his lungs. So why shouldn't he worry that, once the winter sets in, even shit will freeze as it comes out.

Eddie turns his eyes from the perimeter to his hands, moving his numbing fingers carefully and slowly. In the barracks, they talk of a man who came in to breakfast after night duty with his fingers so frozen that they broke as he picked up a mug of tea. "So loud that you could hear them crack, like breaking dry wood." Eddie resists pushing his gloved hands into his armpits as he remembers the storyteller laughing in the barracks. "He carried on raising his hand to his mouth, again and again, till he noticed. He was so cold that he didn't even feel them break." Eddie shivers at his post, unsure if he should believe the story, but he isn't taking any chances.

Patrols are the other thing he doesn't like to think about. Those jagged peaks hide the enemy even in bright sunshine. Eddie peers back past the lights, knowing he stands exposed to a sniper who has the cover of darkness on his side, the liberty to disappear into these mountains, or perhaps into one of the villages beyond. The villages almost seem familiar, with small houses with sheep and cattle all huddled together behind run-down walls. But when he goes through the streets, every sense alert for infiltrators, militants, terrorists, his heart pounding in his chest so loudly that he is sure it can be heard a mile away, he can barely breathe. They stay in formation, following orders, completing the assigned tasks as speedily as they can and returning to base. He refuses to look at any of the villagers he encounters, has grown to hate the shadowy doorways that occasionally fill with miserable, blank-faced people, who stare at the patrols, at him, as if he is the enemy.

Sometimes on a clear day, when he can see for miles, he looks to the east, imagining the rolling greens of the mountains he has called home all his life. He thinks of the market stalls with their stacks of wide taro leaves, of the whitewashed church on the hill where the preacher told them of hell. Eddie had long thought of hell as hot and dry, like the plains. But in the past few weeks, he has learned better.

* * *

As a teenager, Majid learned to keep his head low, to keep his hands visible and prepared to rapidly rise in surrender, and to never make eye contact with the soldiers. These are skills he hopes he will never have to teach another child.

His mother would tell him she was grateful that he never gets angry like the other boys. Majid never broke her heart by telling her that she was wrong, or at least, she was wrong after that day, after he had just turned fourteen.

That was the day a new bunch of soldiers had moved up to the mountain on the other side of the pass. Majid had watched the convoys cross, the Jonga at the front followed by a long line of olive-green three-ton trucks. He had perched on his favourite rock, on a seat high above the road, alternating between gazing idly at the vehicles on the road and checking on his goats, which grazed on the sparse tufts of grass along the slopes.

It had been warm that day, he remembers, with the sun high in a sky without a single cloud. Just an expanse of endless, dizzying blue. As a light breeze fluttered through his hair and the sun tingled on the back of his neck, Majid had felt a deep, calm joy. Perhaps that is why he had let his head fall back against the rock and closed his eyes, not to sleep but to let himself sink into the quiet.

It is why the sudden gunshots sent him tumbling down the rock and onto the gravel below. Rolling to his hands and knees, he had peered down at the road where the convoy had drawn to a halt, the soldiers scrambling to take positions. Shouted orders floated up, too faint for him to understand.

Majid had backed away slowly, still on his hands and knees, dropping into a rocky crease and then hurriedly gathering up his little herd to lead them home. He had told Ammi that there was soldier trouble in the pass and she had praised him for leaving quickly, for bringing the goats home safe.

He had been milking the goats when army trucks screamed into the village over a week later. It was still early morning, the time when chores needed completing, before the men left for work, before Majid picked up the lunch Ammi made him and headed out with the herd. He had finished the milking, returning with an only half-filled pail to Ammi when the soldiers had spotted him.

When they shouted at him, he had frozen. "Hazzup, hazzup . . ." Their voices seem to reach his ears as if through a blizzard, muffled and broken. He knew they were near, stomping towards him on their heavy-soled boots, but he just stayed clutching the metal handle, the milk-warmed pail snug against his knee. "Hazzup," one of the soldiers had yelled, close enough for spittle to land on Majid's cheeks.

He had stared at them unblinking, his limbs growing heavier, the air caught in his chest, until he felt a blow to the back of his legs. His knees had buckled and he had fallen, the milk spilling as the pail crashed to its side, its curved handle still clutched in his hand.

Another hard blow landed between his shoulders. And then more, until he was sprawled on the ground, his cheek pressed into a milky puddle. Somewhere beyond the blizzard in his mind, he could hear Ammi screaming.

Then a boot kicked his hand, the one still clenched around the handle of the milk pail. Kicked again. A soldier bent down and pried open his fingers, forcing his hand open, then someone had pulled him up to his knees. Before him a soldier loomed, the barrel of his weapon pointed at the spot just between Majid's eyes. He had lowered his eyes, watching the boots kneading the spilled milk into mud. "Hazzup!"

A soldier grabbed Majid's arms and pulled them up in the air. "When we tell you, you raise them. And you keep them up till we tell you to put them down. Hazzup! You understand?!"

Majid had finally nodded, not because he understood but because saying yes seemed better. He kept his eyes on the ground, tears building in his eyes as he thought of the spilled milk. And he'd held his hands in the air until the soldiers had left, until the fog in his mind cleared enough to let him hear the bells tinkling on the goats, until a weeping Ammi had pushed his arms down and gathered him to her as if he were still a little child.

They had stayed like that for a long time, kneeling on the milk-wet ground. Ammi had praised him for being calm, being level-headed. She had put healing leaves on his back and borrowed milk from the neighbours to prepare tea for him. "You can't get angry, my son. You can't give them a reason," she had begged.

Majid had nodded, his face buried in her shoulder. He knows boys who get angry. Who go across the border. Who sometimes come back. Boys who are hurt and killed, boys who hurt and kill. He doesn't want to be angry. He doesn't want to leave Ammi and the goats and the rock on the mountain, where the sky is so blue and vast and yet so close that he can almost touch it.

Most days, Majid is glad that he buried Ammi without letting her see the rage that simmers inside him. But some days, he is not so sure.

* * *

Eddie can feel the excitement ripple through the platoon as he rechecks his gear. After six weeks of patrolling grimly silent villages and standing on endless freezing guard duty, his section finally has a task.

Somebody said terrorists had shot at the captain's convoy as it entered the final pass. Eddie was at the gates, scanning the gathering dusk when the vehicles had come screaming up the road, the dust behind them forming a big dark cloud. Word had raced through the camp even before the gates swung open, and the unit had already been in position, rifles loaded and cocked, alert behind sandbags and concrete barriers.

No one had spotted the sniper, nor had there been any damage to man or machine, but Captain Sahib's face was dark with rage, his eyes traced with red. He had fumed and paced in front of the fire, but there was little to be done at night. Nothing beyond the perimeter was safe, so the guard had been strengthened for the night and word had come to be ready before dawn.

Eddie's stomach churns as he joins his section outside for orders. It's the coldest hour of the night, just before dawn, and he shivers as he stands to attention, his eyes looking ahead and into the dark beyond. He wishes he could be elsewhere, could be home, could even be back in his sleeping bag in the barracks behind him. It's a sortie, the havildar tells them, just to the village at the end of the pass, a visit to ensure the villagers understand that this platoon, their company, their regiment, will not stand for any misbehaviour. This morning before the sun climbs in the sky, they will put the fear of god and of their regiment into anyone who dares to threaten them, to shoot at their Captain Sahib.

As he swings up onto the back of the three-tonner, he catches a glimpse of the officer, who wears an expression that Eddie has seen before. That clenched jaw, that gleam in the eye, that twist of the lips takes Eddie back to another time, to a time when all he wanted was to race his brother up the hill, to a time before things went wrong. Nausea rises as he sits down on the wooden bench, staring down as polished boots, oiled weapons and warm bodies fill up the back of the truck. He refuses to look up, even when someone makes a joke about blooding the kids and everybody laughs. They think he's just scared for his first mission and somebody pats his shoulder. Eddie can't manage a grin through the growing sickness.

* * *

It is late when Majid hears about Captain Sahib's rage at the camp. News has a way of travelling up the slopes and down the passes, flying from one mouth to another in whispers as soft as the breeze. He knows it doesn't matter if there was a sniper or a bullet. He knows the soldiers will come to the village at dawn.

But for now, the night is dark as he stands in the doorway, letting the cold seep into his veins, his very bones. Majid knows most of the village is awake in the unlit homes, behind the wooden winter shutters, that the quiet is that of fear, of what the morning shall bring. He can hear the occasional tinkles of bells on goats and sheep. Even though he knows better, knows that the cattle have bedded down for the night, he listens for the deeper clanging of the heavy bell that hangs on his prize bull.

This night, he is grateful again that Ammi is no longer here for him to worry over. He gazes up at the stars, all the brighter seen through eyes that are beginning to tear up from the chill. On the coldest days, when the wind cuts through clothes and skin like knives and the soldiers prefer to stay in their camp, he wishes for someone else to worry over, a wife, even children. But when the spring thaw sets in, he grows afraid that the rage he has banked for so long would be harder to suppress if he also had to worry about a wife, about children. On the summer days, when the ground is soft and warm as a bed, he grows afraid that one day he would need to teach his child to lower his eyes, to raise his hands. He stares at the sky held up by the jagged peaks until he can no longer be sure if it is rage or fear that makes him dizzy. But it is winter still, and something hollow gnaws at his belly, a need for warmth, not of body but some other kind.

Majid had gone down to the valley far below the day after burying Ammi in search of that warmth. He had stayed there long years, working with his hands and mind, learned to operate machines he had not even known existed. He had learned the glimmer of the lake that shone in the sun, dotted with boats larger than his house, and pretty with carved windows and balconies, and followed the leaves of booyn trees turning red and gold and amber. He had made money and saved it, and he had dreamt many dreams and abandoned them.

Finally, just months ago, he had accepted what he had long denied. That valley of green grass and tall trees was not cold enough. The peaks that lined its edges were not the crags that held up his sky. He had missed the cold that sank into his lungs, that nibbled at his fingers as he milked the goats at dawn, that settled deep into his bones and steadied his limbs.

It is why he has used up his savings for the bull that is now bedded down for the night. It is a magnificent beast with brown patches on white, promising the bountiful milk production of the imported cow and the mountain hardiness of the local sire. Majid has already made good money in just the months since he acquired it. And he has big plans for the money that the bull will make him. Plans for repairing Ammi's house, of building a bigger barn, of maybe buying his own milk cow. He has plans of making a home that he can offer a wife, where children can grow, when the hollow in his belly will finally be filled.

As the dawn inches near Majid finds himself lingering in the shed, his eyes accustomed enough to the dark to be able to see the shapes of his goats and sheep in their pens, the heavier, darker smudge of the bull in his newly built stall. It is warm with the body heat of his goats and sheep, and the bull. The occasional draught that sneaks past the reinforced wooden planks is almost welcome, at least to Majid. But he knows it is too cold to take the bull out to the woods beyond the village, too cold to even take the animal out of the stall that Majid has carefully lined with burlap sacks and straw. So he waits, drawing warmth from all that he cares for.

As the light creeps into the shed and the shapes turn to beings, Majid knows that on this day, the persistent gnawing in his stomach is fear.

* * *

The last memory Eddie has of his brother is of terror and sorrow. Edwin and Edgar, almost twins but not quite because Eddie's brother was less than a year older, but acted as responsible as their father. Nobody shortened Edwin's name, as if even as a child, he was too adult for such frivolities. Except when they raced up the hill from school. Then Edwin would laugh and shout and leap to catch an overhanging branch, his smile too big for his face.

Eddie's memory of his father is of his slow breaking, of the dimming of his eyes and his incessant tears. Of a back that never fully straightened after that day in the cemetery. But most of all, Eddie's memory of Father – still living yet no longer alive, back in the green hills – is of a man desperate, pleading and humiliated. It is why he refuses to think about how his brother fell ill, first with fever, then the sweats and shudders, and finally the wrenching spasms, till Father had sent Eddie out from the room and bolted the door shut.

Sometimes he thinks that he should not have accompanied Father to the army check post during those three days. That he should have buried his fears for his ailing brother, who had been wrapped in stinking blankets, constantly sweating and shuddering, clutched tightly in their father's arms. Father had begged the soldiers to help get Edwin to the hospital in the city, to at least give him a pass to get to the big road where buses ran, to do anything at all to help. Eddie had watched as another man with shiny stars on his shoulders had come to the gate, had spoken gruffly to his father to send him away.

Again and again, and through those days and nights, Father had carried Edwin to the check post. With each trip, Edwin's spasms seemed to double, the stench of blood and sweat and rot from the blankets around him multiplied. Finally, his brother had clenched his jaw, his lips stretched as though in a monstrous smile, unable to even drink spoonfuls of water as he thrashed and convulsed in Father's arms.

That last time, Father had wept before the soldiers, kneeling on the dirt before the gate. But that time he did not plead for transport to the hospital. He begged the man with stars on his shoulders for a bullet. "My son is dying. He is in too much pain, please. He will not see the morning but please save him from the pain."

Eddie remembers the man's face as Father knelt before him. He had watched in growing terror as the man had clenched his jaw tight, a strange cruel gleam creeping into his eyes. His fingers had seemed to crawl up to his holster almost of their own accord as he stared at Father. Then one of the other soldiers had whispered to him, urgent and determined. The light had died in the man's eyes. His hand had slid from the holster and risen to the stars on his shoulder. The lips had twisted further as he ran a finger over the epaulette before flinging some words at Father and walking away.

Eddie had been scared enough to keep looking back as they brought Edwin home. He had watched in silence as Father had laid his brother on the bed. He had looked over his shoulder even as Father gently led him to the door, nudged him through it, and closed it shut. He had waited there, his eyes clenched tight, his head against the door, listening to moans and shrieks, sobs and groans.

It had been nearly dawn when his father had emerged, his eyes blank, his shoulders slumped. The dao hung loosely from his fingertips, its blade clean and shiny against the damp dark of his clothes. In the room beyond, there was silence from the soaked, stinking blankets. And there was no Edwin.

* * *

The sun hasn't risen past the eastern peaks when Majid joins the rest in the middle of the village. Two big army trucks block the ends of the road. Soldiers have herded the villagers to the centre.

Majid's hands had risen quickly towards the sky when he had spotted the first soldiers. He breathes deep as he hears shouts of 'Hazzup,' watching out of the corner of his eye as some of the other men are pushed and prodded. He keeps his arms raised as a fresh-faced young soldier with wary eyes pats him down for weapons.

The soldiers pushed everyone towards the small square near the mosque, near a raised stone platform where on other days, children played, and men gathered to sip tea in the evenings. Majid sees the captain standing on the platform, his face is hard like stone, but his eyes glisten.

Beyond the huddled people, Majid can hear the sounds of soldiers searching homes, thuds of furniture knocked over, the clanging of pans dropped to the floor, the shattering of something breakable. Across the square, the young soldier who had searched him looks ready to cry.

The captain began to shout, spittle flying into the air, like one of the villains in the films Majid has seen back in the valley, like the ones on his neighbour's television. He tells the village that he will not lose any of his men in these mountains. He spits out the word *mountain* like a slur. He tells them that he and his men are Naga, famed head-hunters, and not weaklings from the plains. Majid wonders how that is possible, because the young officer looks nothing like the soldiers, seems more like the men from beyond the valley of the lake – men of the plains. He sneaks a peek at the baby-faced soldier, who looks furious at his officer's words.

As his heart thuds ever louder, the strange blizzard Majid remembers from his boyhood builds in his mind, muting the captain's words. He keeps his head lowered, his eyes fixed on the ground before him. Until the heavy clanging of a familiar bell cuts past the muffling in his ears. Two soldiers have led his prize bull into the square. He starts but a gun barrel pushes into his chest, nudging him back amongst the crowd. The soldiers tether the bull, then lash its legs together and pull it to the ground. Majid closes his eyes, dreading what he knows must follow.

On the platform, the captain has pulled out a strange-shaped knife from a sheath, the flat blade widening at the tip. He jumps off the platform, landing on the packed dirt on light feet.

"You see, if we lose one of ours, the next time it will not be an animal, but one of you," he screams, his voice rising to a strange high pitch. Silence falls, followed by a rapid flurry of steps. Then the square is filled with the agonised squeals of Majid's prize bull.

Majid squeezes his eyes shut tighter. He thinks of Ammi, of the promises he made her about staying alive, of his own dreams of a life that seem to grow fainter with each screech of his bull.

Across the square, Eddie forces himself to scan the crowd, to not look at the animal thrashing in pain in the centre of the square. He dares not look at the faces of the silent villagers, and searches instead for movement and body language, for any sign of weapons, of any hint of danger. Eddie pretends not to hear the dying shrieks, until slowly, excruciatingly slowly, the sounds grow fainter and the death spasms turn to twitches.

A strangled, choking sound stops his gaze at a man he intuitively knows is the owner of the dying beast. There is something about the slump of the shoulders, the bow of the head. There is no reason why the man with the wide light eyes should remind Eddie of Father. He is perhaps just a few years older than Eddie, his curling hair the

148

colour of the chocolate bars in their rations. Except Eddie knows that defeated curve of the spine, the humiliation that lies heavy on the rounded shoulders. He also knows the weight of the dao, the swishing sound it makes as it slashes through the air. His throat feels choked with something that rises from deep within his belly and burns up into his mouth and nose. Shame, terror, sorrow and rage, all restrained behind his gritted teeth. Narrowing his eyes, Eddie wills the defeated man to look up.

The bull finally grows still, a circle of blood etched around it in the dirt. As the silence turns to murmurs and the sun begins to pull itself above the eastern peaks, Majid slowly raises his head. His cheeks are wet but his eyes are ablaze.

When Majid's eyes finally meet Eddie's, neither looks away.

Friday Morning Coffee

She is not blessed. She is not fortunate. She is not grateful.

Nusreta's frown deepens and her eyes crinkle up at the edges as she stares at the three empty coffee cups placed in a neat row in front of her. Two are of the same size. Small, barely able to hold a few moderate sips. The delicate pale porcelain gleams in the dusk.

On her left, a cup with deep blue flowers climbing all over it, from the narrow base over the flaring sides, almost over the lip. Ilda would have run her slender finger compulsively over the blossoms, the ragged edge of her chewed nail dragging over the indentations in the pattern. The white is nearly translucent and as she squints, Nusreta thinks she can see the nearly indigo rose on the far side, its shape just discernible. That one is intact, perfect, unlike its partner on the side closest to her. This rose has an ugly smudge of a non-descript shade running through its furled petals. Each Friday, she wonders if she could scrub the mark away, perhaps with a bit of bleach? But she fears that any attempt to remove it will also scrub away the pattern. Perhaps some things that have been dirtied cannot be cleansed? Perhaps they should be left half-hidden under the rubble and filth? That is how she had found Ilda, in the wreckage of her home, a severed arm visible in the ruins, the gold bracelets gleaming in the dirt. Of course, she had known it was Ilda, would have known her neighbour, her friend, her dearest's long-fingered hand as well as her own.

They met every Friday, though Ilda would wave and shout greetings from afar as she rushed back and forth to university, to her knitting circle, to the many, many things that filled up her life during the week. "You get rid of that husband, draga, and you'll see how much you'll find to keep you busy," she'd laugh, strong and loud. Most things Ilda did were strong and loud, but Nusreta knew where she was soft, when she was quiet.

"You'll never find a husband if you don't slow down to at least notice the men who cross your path every day," she tells Ilda as they sit together on the porch, the coffee grown cold between them, the bowl of rahat lokum steadily depleting as they suck on the sugared cubes.

"And who wants a husband? You have one, that is enough for both of us." Ilda grins, sticking out her tongue before pulling it back in to scrape off gummy bits of the sweet from the roof of her mouth. She winks at Nusreta, the setting sun dancing gold in her hazel eyes.

* * *

Afterwards, Nusreta finds work translating, for journalists, for aid workers, for war experts, for peace specialists. "Your English is so good," each one of them tells her, even though she knows it isn't. But then it isn't their language either, and if she pays attention, she catches their idiosyncrasies: the odd syntax of the fresh-faced Dutch volunteers; the double negatives of the French-Canadian negotiators, the loud curses of the American aid workers. "This is a deeply traumatised population," the British station chief tells a newly arrived group. She has shiny, swishy golden hair, the kind that would have made Ilda envious. "So be careful. Be sensitive to their trauma."

"What about me? Who will be careful with me?" Nusreta wants to shout from the corner, where she sits translating yet more victim testimonies. But she knows she is invisible here, that it's better to remain so, that invisibility brings its own protection.

"And for god's sake, stay away from the women. They'll tell you they are traumatised and then bleed you dry. Money is the least of it. They want that passport, not you, remember that!" the station chief warns the men. Nusreta flinches at the words, even though she has been waiting for the now-familiar warning. The men who come to rebuild, to teach peace, always seem too young, clean-shaven, wide-eyed with a kind of naivete that she can't imagine. "Boys, not men, and not even that," Alija's voice grumbles in her ear. As clear and deep and alive as the day he disappeared. She tells herself that he just left, that he found a lover, that he was never in the places where they took the men and boys and shot them all.

The voices fade as she clenches her jaw to push down the rage, forcing herself to remain silent, to stay invisible. She stiffens her legs, tightening them till they become like boards, as hard as the wooden chair she sits on. She turns herself into stone, concentrates on her refusal, her veto, her denial. Her inner, screaming, perpetual, silent No!

Breathe. No.

Close eyes. No.

Clench teeth. No.

"And this is our translator. Her English is very good." Her head snaps up, an automatic smile slashed across her cheeks, then drops down again. She has learned to make it seem like a greeting because it lets her return to invisibility.

She closes her hands into fists, chewed nails digging into her palms, until she can also tamp down the nausea that they tell her is normal for women in her condition. She wishes she could say no again.

* * *

The one in the centre is simple, with no pattern, but its colour is a deep dark red that gleams and glimmers in the dim light of this land. Nusreta isn't sure who drank from it but she found it discarded at the sink on her last day of work, the day before she left forever. There is a tiny chip at the base, pale in the enamel, and startling like a broken bone pushed out of bloodied flesh. She covers it each time she picks it up, running her finger pad over the roughness, against the open wound in the swirl of crimson.

"In the end they are men," Ilda had comforted her as the war grew closer. The distant rumble of the day before had turned into a deafening roar, a continuous cacophony of guns and explosions and crumbling homes and offices and schools. They had both grown deaf to all but the newest of the heavy guns, their rapid familiarity with horror becoming a horror in itself. "They are just men. You can survive men." Ilda's teeth had flashed suddenly, bright in the gloom of the basement. "Unlike these guns."

Alija had been frantic, trying to find a way out for her, for Ilda too. Overnight, the rumours had turned to shouts, which would soon become screams. In a matter of hours, not days, the rumours would also grow true. But that night there was just the shuddering booms of explosions that grew closer by the minute. "You stay together," Alija had told them, made them promise. "Keep Ilda with you," he'd whispered. Then, once he'd heard her lock and bolt the door, he pushed it with his hand, and then his entire weight, to check that it would hold.

It was nearly dawn when Ilda had turned in her arms, pushing herself away. The explosions had receded towards the hills, the quiet periods between the booms elongating like torturously held breaths. "Alija will be back soon," Nusreta had whispered, unwilling to let go just yet.

"We ate all the rahat lokum. I'll get some. I bought a big batch the day before yesterday."

Nusreta had clutched at the beloved long-fingered hand, her own cold and clammy against its warmth.

"You wait here. I'll get them from home. Alija will be so surprised."

Nusreta's eyes prickled until Ilda's face had grown blurred.

"Stay here. I'll be right back."

A creak of the step at the top of the stairs. A brief sliver of light as the cellar door opened, a shadow slipped out, and gloom returned. She doesn't know when the explosions had neared again, when the heaviest guns had resumed their barking, or when she had fallen asleep, finally warm, huddled under all the quilts – hers, Alija's, Ilda's – when she had finally warmed up.

The silence had woken her. And the warmth. Her nose was full of scents that she loves: Ilda's floral musk, Alija's coffee and tobacco, something citric that she recognises as her own. The guns were quiet now, preferring to rain down their terror in their dark.

The sun was bright when Nusreta climbed up to the house. It burned hot all afternoon as she swept up the broken glass, the lumps of cement that had fallen off the ceiling, the dust that seemed to bleed out of the very bones of their homes with each shelling. She dusted, and cleaned, and mopped, and scrubbed, until everything was nearly as clean as the day before. She tried not to think of Alija. Or of Ilda.

But Alija didn't return even after the guns stopped firing. He didn't return even after Nusreta ventured out into the dusk to see that Ilda's little house was gone. Not even after she walked around in the rubble, looking for something that had no name. Not even when she found Ilda's arm stretching out into the light from beneath the debris.

Sometimes, only sometimes, Nusreta wishes she had thought to take the bangles.

* * *

The first one is just a child, his cheeks still sprouting fuzz too light to shave. He catches her at the first fall of dark, when she slips out to check on a boarded-up window. Days ago Alija had hammered thick planks across the shutters, but she has been hearing a clacking in the wind all day.

He smiles up at her as she stands on the ladder, her mouth full of nails. She has a hammer in her hand but he keeps looking back over his shoulder to the road where his friends stand, laughing and egging him on. It will make him a man, as if that is all it takes to become a man. She climbs down slowly, silently, and walks him to the long bench in the living room.

He doesn't last long, for which she should be grateful, she thinks. And he is kind or perhaps embarrassed enough to close the door to keep some semblance of privacy. Afterwards, he fixes the loose plank on the window, blushing furiously, before rushing away.

They come in alone, or sometimes in two-s and three-s after that. She learns to lie stiff as a board at first. Then she learns to grit her teeth so hard that her no reverberates like a never-ending echo inside her body, ricocheting like a bullet down to her toes, then back up through her shuddering heart and into her head. In the brief moments she surfaces to herself, she often smells slivovitz on their breaths, at times can taste it in her mouth when they thrust their tongue into her. She wonders if it counts as drinking alcohol. Does this damn her, too?

"It happens to women even in peacetime," Ilda whispers in her ear when she thinks she will break. "Even our men do this to us and nobody does anything." Nusreta draws strength from those whispers, learns to clean her body with rags, her mind with Ilda's words, and her soul with echoes of Alija's affection. Maybe not all men, she argues with the Ilda of her mind, and with herself.

One of them likes being rough, likes to push her till she whimpers, sobs, weeps. She does it all because she has learned that he finishes faster that way. But she also fears that he doesn't just want to take from her, but to break her. "He's done this before," Ilda whispers, "to his own women. Or at least he's wanted to." She doesn't break until he grabs her jaw and forces her to look him in the eye. He thrusts again, grinning as he holds her gaze, tightening his fingers on her jaw, until deliberately, calmly, he spits in her face just as he comes. She shatters after he leaves, wishing she'd had Alija's luck, Ilda's good fortune.

The man with stars on his shoulder, and gold-hazel eyes that remind her of Ilda's, shows up the next morning. He brings oranges in a brown paper bag. He asks her name, talks about the weather. "We all do terrible things in war," he tells her, before removing her shirt. "I am a good man, but even me." She says nothing.

Afterwards he asks for coffee: "The proper way only women make at home." He looks wistful, almost kind. And he tells her that none of the other men will come to her if he likes the coffee. That she will be safe. He pulls out a small bag of fine ground coffee, and rahat lokum that glistens pink in the polythene bag. "You have a real grinder. I will bring beans next time," he offers, seated at her kitchen table as she gathers her things, his eyes wandering over her counters and jars, over the broken dishes piled in the corner, over her. Like it is all his.

She is careful as she boils the water and puts aside some of it in a cup. She adds the ground beans to the now-dulled dzezva and tops it with the boiling water. The fragrance nearly punctures her calm, and she can't stop her fingers from reaching that spot on her belly where she used to hold the grinder, the spot that would ache dully afterwards, where Alija would place a kiss to thank her, where Ilda's fingertips would graze her gently as she scolded her. "Don't press so hard, or the bruise will never fade."

She watches the brew rise to a boil, the foam building steadily, removes it from the flame, then places it back again. Once, twice, thrice. Just like before.

When the foam is full and creamy, the brew below it thick and dark as sludge, she adds a splash of water and brings it to the table to settle. His hazel eyes are lit up, like a little boy re-encountering a favourite toy.

She sets up the rest of the table. A small glass of cool water. A chipped plate for rahat lokum. She scoops a bit of the foam into a cup, then pours a careful, slow, thin stream almost to the rim.

He thanks her, gently holding her hand, as if they are lovers. She hopes he won't notice, that he'll think that she has no other cups. That he will ignore her insult just as he has ignored her unspoken *Noes*. A sliver of a smile crosses her face as she turns away, hearing his satisfied groan behind her. Telling her that he approves of the coffee even though it is served in a woman's cup, one of her own, covered in pretty yellow flowers.

He doesn't deserve a man's cup. None of them do.

* * *

She always places her favourite one, the most loved one on the right. It's the colour of rich cream, like freshly churned butter, with a simple band of gold edging the rim. For Alija. Her friend? Her husband? Her secret-keeper? She no longer knows what he was to her. Some days she wishes she could have saved at least one of the photo albums from their home, because she has forgotten if his eyes were blue on their wedding day or the strange gold-hazel of Ilda's. Some days, she looks into those same eyes in her daughter's face and she forgets to breathe, feels the pain throb fresh, deep within her, until she can bury it again. In those moments, she tells herself that her love's eyes were different to these, that she could never have feared them. She reminds herself of gentle caresses, of giggles smothered with kisses, of moans born only of pleasure.

She lingers over the cream-and-gold fildzan, smaller than the other two. A man's cup. Meant to hold nothing more than two swallows of her strongest brew. Even after all these years, her tongue can nearly taste him when she pours the coffee over the foam. She used to steal a taste from him each time, not enough to count as a sip, but just a wetting of her lip and the tip of her tongue. "Careful, or you'll grow a tail from drinking man's coffee," Alija would tease her, tapping her scrunched-up nose.

"Is that how you men grow yours?" she'd tease back, but only after they had grown accustomed to each other.

"That is men's secret, my love," he'd laugh, pulling her closer. Somewhere inside her, buried deep, she remembers it hadn't hurt with Alija. She knows that in the before, love was pleasure, that her body could come alive with just a hot breathed whisper. That hands and mouths, bodies, even penises, can seek and explore, discover and remember, caress and comfort, excite and satisfy.

The foam rises in the pot and she snatches it off the heat just before it overflows the edges and sets it down to cool. As the foam fades and grounds settle, she moves it back to the heat. Once, twice, thrice. Ilda had taught her to make the coffee the way Alija liked. "He is bitter, you're the sugar. Me? I'm the dzezva that just boils and boils and gets poured out." She remembers that Ilda had sounded happy. Remembers the beauty spot that punctuated the delicate curve of her neck. Remembers the trembling warmth of that skin.

She peers at the foam bubbling over the copper, dips a fingertip in to caress the hot murk and brings it to her mouth. The brew is rich, strong, bitter. Just like Alija loved. For an instant she knows that his eyes were blue, pale like the winter sky. They were not the gold-hazel of her daughter's. But then she catches herself, forces herself to breathe slowly, deeply, until her heartbeat slows to normal.

* * *

Ilda's cup of roses gleams and glimmers in the dim light of this new, quiet, solitary, flat land. It is filled to the brim, and the coffee foam settles into miniscule hills and valleys, serene under echoes of a different, brighter sun. She can see Ilda raise it to her lips, her eyes shining over the rim. Eyes that she sees in her daughter's face, familiar and yet strange. Ilda lives in Aida, in her whorls of chestnut hair, in the careless shrug of her shoulders, in her loud confidence, in her deliberate lack of fear.

She scoops up the foam to spoon it gently into Alija's cup, dredging up the love she feels every time she thinks of her beautiful daughter, raised alone by her in a land that remains foreign to her. Aida carries Alija in her easy grin, in her freely shared affections, the gentle way she cares for Nusreta. The way she never asks, never voices her doubts.

Nusreta never fills the crimson cup in the centre, the one she found abandoned in the rubbish. She runs her finger over the smooth glaze, wonders again who drank from it. Her fingertip runs over the rim, in steady circles. How many drank from this one? Her finger snags where the glaze is chipped. Who broke it? Smudged, abandoned, broken, disappeared. She chokes down a sob as another pair of hazel-gold eyes hover at her memory's edge, colder than Ilda's, not as beloved as Aida's. For an instant she thinks she will fall again, crumble again.

Then the door slams open. "Are you ready, Mama?" Aida takes extra care to make her entry loud, letting her bag fall with a thud, jangling her keys. It's a habit she formed as a child, precociously recognising that some sorrows are best borne alone. Her chatter rises and fades from the hall as she stalls. "You should wear the blue coat today . . . and we are going to a new cafe . . . can you make that cake again for me . . ." Nusreta is grateful for Aida's tender discretion that lets her gather herself once again.

They told her that it's the worst thing that can happen to a woman. But she knows that is untrue. The living tell the stories. The living keep the memories. The living raise the children. And it is the living who choose which stories, memories and names are told to the children. Nusreta knows this. Death is the worst thing that can happen. To anyone. This knowledge has re-knitted her, helped her ensure that Aida is strong, happy, intact. Perhaps, she thinks, that makes her fortunate.

A few deep breaths calm her, stop her hands from shaking. She rises to slowly pour out the cups into the sink, feeding the coffee bitters to the herbs on the window. She smiles at Aida's voice, her words clothed in the accent of this new, foreign land. "I need new boots, Mama. Will you come shopping with me?" The voice is light, bright, the tone joyful, of a young woman who has known little danger, will know no war. And that could be a blessing.

Amidst the Deodars

Vir has taken to walking the grounds of the bungalow every night since his return, though maybe stumbling is a better word, as he leans heavily on the sturdy mahogany cane yet still trips over every pebble, his own toes, even emptiness. Or perhaps "shuffling" is a better description for the slow, wavering, painful steps he is forced to take now.

He refuses to count the steps he must take until he is beyond the front door. Then there are eleven sliding paces across the shaded veranda; four agonising ones down the creaking wooden steps to the garden path. After the first three nights of struggling to grip the red-painted banister and his unwieldy cane, of toppling over and rolling down to the pebbled path, he has developed a better system: he throws the cane down first and then grips the banister with both hands, pushing and pulling his body sideways to make his way down. The manoeuvre still leaves him winded and his arms and shoulders burning, but at least he hasn't fallen down since. Once he manages to pick up his cane and turn right, one hundred and three steps take him to the stone wall just high enough to stop him from flinging himself into the ravine beyond. It's two hundred and three steps along this crumbling barrier which then gives way to the white picket fence that continues around the bungalow. Midway along the wall, where the oldest deodars are clustered, their gnarled branches stretching over the ravine, is an ornate cast iron bench. Vir has taken to resting there, staring in turns at the fog filling the empty abyss, and the winding path leading down the hill beyond the fence.

The first night, he had only managed half a round, crumpling in pain and exhaustion before he could reach the cold iron seat. He had wept then, like a child at first, with big gulping tears. And then like a man who has lost things he knows he should not be so anguished to lose, and yet grieves for them all the same. He had tried to argue himself into living. They're only injuries, he had reminded himself, he would heal to something like he was before. It could be worse, he had told himself, thinking of the blank-faced, teary-eyed widows of those who died in combat. Then, as he had run a finger along the still-angry scar across his face, he had wondered if he had also lost the possibility of an anxious wife who he'd fear to leave a widow. For all that he wants to pull himself together, it is the loss of such possibilities, of his dreams, ambitions, that aches. More, much more, than his damaged leg, his scarred face, his battered body. Finally, staring at the twisting branches far above the ground, he had wished for death.

Despite the shivering, bone-deep cold, he hadn't been grateful when the sky had lightened that morning. He had been still, curled awkwardly on the grass, in a foetal position, his damaged leg jutting out straight. His knee no longer bends without maddening streaks of agony that leave him gasping. He hadn't even tried to move or call for help and had instead stayed on the ground, eyes closed, entirely drained, until the pinja-la had carefully carried him into the house, cleaned and dressed him, and tucked him into a bed warmed by fresh hot-water bottles. He should be grateful that he is cared for, but that too reminds him of all that he has lost, including even the ability to clean and dress himself without pain.

At least this bungalow stands far, far from the rest, so none are likely to hear his furious, pained howls. Even if they did, they would likely think it was the wind amongst the twisted trees. Or one of the many ghosts that supposedly haunt this old cantonment town. After that first night, he has not wept. Instead, each night, he screams into the mist-covered valley, at the sky beyond the looming trees, at the seductive fall beyond the stone wall.

He tells himself he should be glad that he is billeted in this isolated bungalow, set further up the hill from the others, where he needs only manage the four steps to the mostly flat garden to shout his despair into the deodars. Unmarried officers like him usually room at the mess, closer to the headquarters at the top of the hill. But that can only be reached by a vehicle, or a horse, or by the long winding footpath that he used to run along every morning in the times before. And then, there are the forty-three steps from the mess to the officers' quarters that he used to love sprinting up, but which he now dares not imagine climbing. Small mercies, he tells himself, on the nights when he has pushed himself to complete a circuit of the garden before collapsing onto the bench. And he tries to hold on to that fragment of comfort.

* * *

"Did we lose again?" Vir is startled by the man squatting on the grass, calmly preparing a wad of chewing tobacco in his palms. He wears a cotton kurta, and loose trousers of some indeterminate colour, both too light to offer any protection from the damp chill. At least he has acquired an incongruous red coat, probably one of the moth-eaten leftovers from the British that are still found in the market in the valley. He's lean and tall, oddly delicate, and when he speaks, his accent is from the plains.

For a moment, Vir wonders if he should ask why the man is in the garden at this hour, whether he should call for guards. But there is something calming about his methodical sifting, patting and shaping of the tobacco into a chewable wad, something stolid in the way he rests on the grass, even a strange kind of elegance to it. "Lose what?" he croaks instead.

"The war. Did we lose again?"

Vir has no answer. They had big celebrations after the surrender documents were signed. The generals congratulated all of them – his country, his army, even strangers. Everyone is sure they won. But have they? Has he?

"They call me a traitor," the man continues, his language a little odd, not enough to be incomprehensible, but just enough to seem out of time. "I fought for the Company for twenty years, for coin, yes, but always loyally. But the first time I fight for myself, they call me a traitor. How can that be treason?"

He calls himself a baghee, Vir notices. A word no longer in much use even in the plains. The war Vir has just fought also began as an uprising. But it wasn't an uprising of his people, in his country. So what did that make him? He wraps his palm carefully around his damaged, aching knee. Had he been fighting for coin, too?

"When we lost Delhi, when the Company captured the Badshah, we ran. I came up to the mountains, even though I had never seen them." The man waves at the valley below that Vir knows stretches to the Shivalik hills, and then beyond to the plains to Delhi. "At first it was only to hide, but then I got used to the cold filling my lungs. I began to love the quiet of these twisted trees, especially when the fog wraps them up." Vir is grateful for the man's soft voice, his gently rolling cadence, and for not being expected to respond. He lets his mind wander, only half-listening to the man tell his tale. "For years, nobody cared that I was here. Then they came to build the cantonment on the hill. Not for the Company they said, but for their queen. They still called us traitors. And they still hated us enough to shoot at us."

In the gathering mist, the man's coat appears more battered, darkened along his left side as if wet. The cotton shirt underneath is stained too, as if by rust or blood. As Vir watches the man tuck the carefully prepared wad of tobacco into the side of his mouth, he thinks the mist must be getting heavier. The man is harder to see in the thickening fog, the grey swirls swallowing him rapidly. His voice fades to a whisper. "I thought I began losing when I started to fight for myself. But maybe I was lost all along."

* * *

"Has Death come back with you?" the child shouts at Vir from beyond the fence. She comes up the winding path most afternoons, lingering beyond the small, latched gate. Major Thambe's daughter seems impossibly small, although Vir has little idea of children. She giggles and jumps and clambers up the tree trunks, but her eyes remain shadowed and solemn. She stares at him with that unabashed curiosity that is, sometimes viciously, taught out of small children. He doesn't know how to answer.

"I see Ruchi has adopted you," the major tells him when he comes in to check on him that evening. "She has a fancy that Death lives in this bungalow." Vir wants to shout at him, tell him to go away, to go and find his pretty lady wife and his wide-eyed, too serious daughter, to leave him alone. He takes a deep breath to clear the rage from his mind and nods, but the major has turned away, moving to gaze out of the casement window, a finger tracing the diamond-patterned panes.

"We came here, once. Ruchi and I. She wanted to trap the rain clouds." His voice has lightened to something almost like it had been months ago. "It was before . . ." He trails off, and Vir doesn't need any further explanation. Before they marched to war, before the empty spaces in their ranks, before the homes on these hills were emptied of mutilated families. Major Thambe gives his head a firm brief shake as if to clear it. "Don't worry. I'll tell that little scamp to not annoy you."

Vir inwardly groans at the realisation that the major has no intention of stopping his child's visits. "You shouldn't let her wander about on her own," he suggests.

"She's not alone. Gompo-la follows her everywhere, but she doesn't know that. My wife thinks it's better, teaches her independence."

He should have realised that. That old soldier-monk seems to be on his way to adopting him, too. Vir has seen him light the Petromaxes every night after dinner and place them strategically around his garden route. On clear nights, they light up much of the path, leaving only patches of lurking shadows under the deodars. On misty nights, they are dimmed beacons as he pushes himself to cover more ground. On those nights he counts them, ensuring that he avoids the ones placed on the stone wall next to the ravine, seeking out the ones that lead him to the pines, then under the canopy of the six apple trees, behind the kitchen and past the vegetable patch, between the old deodars beyond the fence, and then back to the pebbled path to the front door.

Gompo-la is older than the others, a ranking officer of that army in exile that, by some irony of politics, is now also Vir's to lead, if not fully command. He came over when the leaders of his government were forced to flee over the mountains. Vir doesn't quite understand whether he was a monk, or a soldier, or some combination of the two, but he knows not all of Gompo-la's family made it to safety. He has a brother, two nephews and a son who all serve in Vir's unit, two of them in his own company. They are steely-eyed men with near-identical although rare smiles, who fight with a ferocity that Vir knows comes from a personal sorrow that he, the professional soldier, does not comprehend. Vir knows one of those men was injured alongside him, that he too was airlifted back to the base. He feels shame that he has not thought of that man, nor of any of his men, in the past weeks.

* * *

The tinkling bells on her ankles announce her arrival long before he sees her emerge from the mists. Burnished bangles glitter impossibly on her wrists. Tarnished gilt thread shines in the drapes of the heavily embroidered but faded ghaghra that swishes with her every step. The first night he saw her balance on the narrow stone wall, her arms held out wide over the steep fall, Vir had almost called out a warning. Then she had twirled, not with the elegance of a dancer, but with the surety of a woman who knows her own appetites.

"Do you have need of me, sahib?" she had called out, her voice warm with laughter, smooth and lush like fresh honey. He had looked away instead, his cheeks warm with embarrassment. She had chortled then, teasing, even mocking, but not cruel, before mincing along the crumbling stone barrier and disappearing past the deodars.

"Are you sure you don't have work for me?" she asks him this night. She is sitting on the wall, legs dangling over the ravine, head thrown back so that her long ribboned braid hangs almost down to the flower bed below.

He has grown so accustomed to encountering visitors on his nightly rounds that he barely even starts. Instead, he moves off the path, feeling the flagstones give way to softer soil under his cane, then his feet, until he can lean against the chilled stones. "There is nothing you can do for me," he mumbles.

Up close, she is beautiful, with eyes that are brown and green with gold flecks, and a rich golden tone to her skin. Her hair gleams in the moonbeams that filter through the fog-shrouded deodars. Not from the hills, he thinks, even though she sounds local.

"I am fourth generation, from the pink house, in the bazaar." She grins at him. "I can do things you can't even imagine." His face grows warmer at her wink as he realises what she is offering. Maybe before he would have accepted, but now, he can't think of women without remembering what he saw over there, in the prisons and fields, villages and camps.

He begins to straighten up, pushing himself to leave, but she laughs. "We can also just talk, sahib." Her braid swishes near his cane and her breath seems warm against his ear. He nods and settles back against the wall, near enough this time that he can smell jasmine and smoky pine and musk on her.

"They call me Sona, because I am all gold," she tells him, waiting till he looks at her. She leans back and turns her head to bare an expanse of neck under her shawl. "It's like that all over, sahib." Her voice is soft, full of promise. "Or maybe it's for all the gold that the officers like to spend on me." Her laughter is harsh this time, but the sound is quickly swallowed by the abyss.

"I used to meet him here," she confides, drawing his gaze up the quaint choli that looks like something out of old photographs. "The gora sahib who loved me, even wanted to marry me. Every night, we met like this. He was shy too, just like you. But then he had to go to fight in England, in the big war. When we met to say goodbye that last night, he said that he was selfish, that he never wanted another man to have me." The tinkling bells on her ankles have fallen silent, and all mischief and seduction have drained from her still body.

"Love is dangerous, sahib, even deadly. Maybe more than war," she whispers, not seductive any more, just pained. Even as he begins to fully turn to her, she rises abruptly to her feet, scrambling up on her hands and knees on the narrow ledge, then balances precariously on the jagged stones, her ghaghra flaring out over the void.

175

Vir reaches out to steady her, but she's already beyond his fingertips.

* * *

Ruchi comes closer to the bungalow with each visit, initially just to carefully unlatch the green gate and observe him in silence before leaving. At first, she stands at a spot close to the gate but then grows confident enough to meander closer to the bungalow. She's quiet, oddly self-contained and unfailingly polite. She always says hello when she arrives, and calls out a hasty goodbye, latching the gate behind her, when she leaves. Vir waits till she's down the road before he lets the ends of his mouth curl up. It would be a smile, he thinks, but with the still-livid scar running across his cheek and down to his jaw, it may just twist his face into something grotesque.

With each visit, she makes her way closer to the edge of the veranda, stepping carefully in the flower beds that Gompo-la tends so diligently. Her purple shirt is almost the same colour as the wild irises that are in bloom there. Vir ignores her humming and soft whispers to herself, refusing to offer any sign of friendliness, preferring to lose himself in his own thoughts until he notices that she has fallen silent.

When he turns his head, Ruchi is staring at him, her small face pushed against the heavy wooden posts that hold up the banister. She looks like she wants to cry, but then she purses her wobbling lip and squares her little shoulders. "Do you know Gompo-la's son died?"

Vir can't remember if he was informed. "His name was Tashi. He died bravely." Something in her tone makes him think she's repeating the words of an adult, perhaps her mother. Vir wonders if they would have said the same of him. A part of him wishes he knew what to tell her, another wishes she would leave. He settles for looking away, staring at the chasm beyond the garden, seeking the jagged blue peaks in the far distance.

But Ruchi is a persistent child, and moves through the flower bed and along the perimeter of the veranda until she is squarely in front of him, her face again pressed against the balusters. "Father says Death can't get me. That he'll always protect me. But Gompo-la couldn't protect Tashi-la, so maybe Father is wrong?" There is a little furrow between her eyes as she puzzles over that possibility.

Vir feels like he should say something, but does not know whether to offer her comfort or truth. His voice is scratchy, his words stilted. "Fathers can only try, but . . ." He stops, confused both by his attempt to talk, and his inability to say anything meaningful.

But that seems to be enough for Ruchi, who nods knowingly. "I know Father will try his best."

He has grown so accustomed to her visits that he barely notices when she climbs up the four steps to the edge of the veranda. "I came here before Father marched with all of you. I locked Death in so he couldn't march with Father, with the pinja-la, with all of you. But he escaped somehow."

His surprise makes him turn away from the mists gathering on the peaks above. Ruchi stands on the top step of the veranda, her frail arm wrapped around a heavy baluster. Her face is scrunched into the scowl that he has learned means that she is thinking.

"Maybe, now you live in this bungalow, Death has other quarters?"

* * *

"You see them, don't you?" Vir spots Gompo-la only after he has come to rest on the hard wrought iron bench. The older man stands under the largest deodar, engulfed almost entirely in the growing mist, and so still that he seems to blend into the dark tree trunk. "I know they come visit you."

Vir can do nothing but nod in affirmative.

"My Tashi is twenty-two, six feet tall, about sixty kilos, and has a scar just above his left eyebrow." Vir nods again, knowing that these words could apply to many men. "He has laughing eyes," Gompo-la adds in a whisper, the clinical description giving way to the memories of a grieving father. "He was a happy baby, has grown into a happy man."

Vir holds out his hand, indicating the empty space on the bench, inviting the man to sit beside him. Tendrils of mist cling to Gompo-la as he steps away from the tree, unfurling their grasp slowly as he nears the bench. His voice is low. "My son held on till they brought him back, until I could look at him again. Maybe he needed to tell me something."

Gompo-la seats himself not on the bench, but cross-legged on the damp grass below, leaning his head against the ornate wrought iron seat. His left hand clutches a carnelian threngwa, its smooth beads running like drops of blood through his fingers. He steadies himself with long, deep breaths, and settles into a pattern of caressing each stone of the garland between his thumb and index finger for a moment before moving on to the next. His voice takes on the familiar soothing rhythm, his words rising and falling in the gentle cadence Vir has grown to know well. "Tashi was always like that, stubborn. When we came over the mountains, he was young, but he still insisted on walking all the way himself. I would wait for him and let the others go ahead because he would fall so far behind on the path. But he made me promise never to go back for him. He told me that he would catch up. And he did, every single night."

Love swirls through the words, in Gompo-la's deep voice, until Vir finds himself envying the dead man. It is an emotion he hadn't known before, but he now seems to envy almost everyone, the dead, the living, but most of all anyone who is whole enough to love, to be loved. He wonders if his father, far away in the plains, speaks of him in this way, full of love and sorrow, pride and longing. He knows they would have received the news by telegram. Perhaps an officer stationed at the cantonment would have been kind enough to deliver the news personally. Vir knows which he prefers.

They sit like that in the dark as one by one, the Petromaxes dim and go out. Vir slumps further down on the hard bench, listening in his half-sleep to stories that run into each other. Sometime in the night, Gompo-la runs out of words and switches to the chant that accompanies his gentle worrying of the carnelian beads.

Om mani padme hum.

"I would like to see my son again. Even if he is scarred or in pieces, I would like to see him, just once, laughing like before." Vir startles into wakefulness at the change in Gompo-la's voice. The sky is just beginning to lighten beyond the eastern peaks. Despite the chill and discomfort, he feels strangely rested. Near him, on the grass, Gompo-la is seated as before, cross-legged. His face, even in profile, is serene, although a single moist track runs from the edge of a closed eye down to his jaw and beyond. Vir searches for words to offer in comfort but the older man holds up a hand. "I wish to see him, but I think my son completed all he had to do in this life. I should be happy for him . . . but perhaps I am too selfish."

He does not look up as Vir stands and makes his way stiffly, painfully, back into the bungalow.

Perhaps that is why Vir is surprised when he sees Gompo-la walk up the twisting path with Ruchi late that afternoon, the child guarding a brown paper bag in her arms. The two of them are deep in conversation, and Vir knows it's about him. They stop beyond the fence, staring at his bungalow yet refusing to acknowledge him as he waits in his usual armchair. They remind him of soldiers summoning up their courage before a battle.

Eventually, Gompo-la unlatches the gate and nods at Ruchi to step forward, then latching the gate again behind her. She hesitates at the steps, before squaring her shoulders and squinting, her tiny, determined face suddenly much like her father's. "I asked Mommy for jam biscuits for us," she announces, starting to climb up the creaking steps. "They're my favourite."

He can't think of anything to say so just nods. She places the paper bag on the table and clambers up to sit in the other chair, her legs dangling over the seat. They sit in silence, which increasingly grows uncomfortable for him. He has no idea what to say to a child, to anyone, really.

"Gompo-la says it worked. Locking Death in here," she finally whispers. "But it didn't work for everyone. Not for his son, not for so many others." Her eyes brighten as she holds out a jam biscuit to him, its centre a glistening blood-red. "But it worked for Father and many pinja-la in the camp . . ." She trails off. Vir stares at the child till she smiles widely. "And it worked for you. We know. Because Death keeps all his favourites here with him."

Previous Places of Publication

'The Tango Bar' as 'A Tango Bar in Buenos Aires' in *The Good Journal*

'In the Vauxhall Pleasure Gardens' in *An Unreliable Guide to London*. London: Influx Press

'The Wait' in *Ellery Queen's Mystery Magazine* (Japanese translation in *Hayakawa Mystery Magazine*)

'Faded Serge and Yellowed Lace' in *World Literature Today*

'Diplomatic Immunity Fatigue' in *The Drawbridge*

'The Tigress Hunts' as 'Tomorrow the Tigress Will Hunt' in *The Drawbridge*

'Number-Nine Bungalow' as 'Bungalow Number Nine' in *Days of Innocence: Stories for Ruskin Bond*, ed. Namita Gokhale. New Delhi: Roli Books

Acknowledgements

I have been writing these stories all my life so first of all, all my love and thanks to my family: to my Dad for gifting us courage, the determination to keep going regardless of odds, and PTSD; my mother for teaching us how to navigate all three of these safely and successfully; Rashmi who continues to unfailingly share her research and unstinting love; and Siddharth who remains my greatest supporter and moral compass.

As ever, immense love and gratitude to my agent Laura Susijn. I can't thank you enough for your patience, care and loyalty.

These stories could not have been written without input from a large number of soldiers and officers, scholars and journalists, activists and healers. You generously shared your knowledge and testimonies with me. You read and re-read drafts, corrected my mistakes with endless patience, and always led me to greater empathy and understanding. Many of you cannot be named here, but you know who you are and you have my endless gratitude. I honour you with this book and shall forever treasure the stories you entrusted to me.

My gratitude to the many officers, soldiers and associates of the Special Frontier Force who first taught me that humour and kindness exist even in times of war. My heartfelt thanks to Ratu Ngawang, Jampa Kalden, and my own Gompo-la, who thought it hilarious that I named a character for him. You are held with great admiration and affection in memory. My respect for Mr. R.N. Kao has grown since our last meeting. Thank you for your frank answers and for listening to my furious *j'accuse* with grace and unexpected empathy.

This story of writing this book is also the story of my political, ethical and literary education. There are many teachers I must honour for their lessons, starting with Chander Mahadev and Fakhru, who were my first introduction to journalism, and how the personal cannot not be separated from the political. My love to Camille Hall, who long ago adopted a bemused teenager in New York, told me to read Malcolm X, and is never surprised when I phone her out of the blue. Huge thanks to Rashmi Singh and Monika Thakur for difficult lessons on working with violence and trauma while centring respect and care. Sinia Jain has long been an essential personal and professional support. Thank you for always boosting morale while creating spaces for conversations with serving officers to speak about much that is painful.

This collection has required me to learn how to balance knowledge, understanding and compassion on and off the page, and I am fortunate to have encountered many teachers who helped me achieve this. My gratitude to Liz Kelly and colleagues at the Child and Woman Abuse Studies Unit at London Metropolitan University for their guidance on how to write about victim-survivors. Prof. Susan Ballyn and Dr. Ana Moya Gutierrez were key to my education in anti-colonial writing and I remain grateful for their lessons. I have endless gratitude for colleagues who have nurtured, shaped, and continue to nourish my understanding of the world: Prof. Heidi Mirza, Prof. Olivette Otele, Sara Ahmed, Dr. Yasmin Gunaratnam, Mary Rambaran-Olm and Ambereen Dadabhoy. I remain in awe of you and your works.

Many extraordinary teachers are essential to my development of an ethical creative and intellectual practice, but I hold Josh Shahryar, Sydette Harry, Amanda Rogers, Flavia Dzodan and Amba Azaad in particular affection and gratitude. Thank you also to Betsy Stang, Sol Hogstrand, Hend Amry, Zehra Zaidi, Neelam Raina and Leah McElrath for teaching me to bear witness, especially when that is all we can do.

There are many experts who have read and re-read my drafts and provided gentle corrections, generous advice and deep insights. The deepest gratitude to Isabella Petith and Andres Garcia for teaching me of Buenos Aires, dictatorship, tango, and love; Nidzara Ahmetasevic who found my description of Bosnian coffee-making surprisingly credible – thank you for your infinite patience and generosity in correcting my many mistakes; Marta Roca, who first spoke to me of the unspoken histories in Barcelona; Antonia Navarro Tejero who provided a safe space for the foreigner to share writings about barely buried traumas and agonising legacies; Edward Wilson who shared his knowledge of covert histories from both sides of the Atlantic; and Trevor Norris whose literary sensibility and criticality, and expertise of French and British literatures, has immeasurably enriched my work.

I am very fortunate to learn from incredible journalists, researchers and chroniclers, many of whom I also count as friends. My abiding affection and thanks to Julia Reinhart, Asteris Masouras, Irfan Master, Sara Salem, Connie Agius, Elizia Volkmann, Shaista Aziz and Roxanna Shapour. Thank you also to Anna Paterson, Azadeh Moaveni and Ramita Navai for your open-hearted insights. My gratitude and love to Meena Kandasamy, Jamilah Ahmed, Jessie Daniels and Soraya Chemaly for constantly enriching my writing, thinking and view of the world. Your empathy, strength and intellectual acuity is an inspiration and model for me. Thank you to Joy Francis, Aki Schilz and Louise Doughty for serendipitously emerging to support and bolster me just when I am reeling. I wish we saw each other more often as I cherish every moment we share.

There are many friends and colleagues who sustain me emotionally, intellectually and creatively, who step up and step in without asking, again and again, even before I know they are needed. My deepest gratitude and love to Kate Birch, Tashmia Owen, Sheri Ahmed, Catherine Rowley-Williams, Glenn Reid, and Kaushik Mitter.

My gratitude to Vidisha Biswas and the absolutely brilliant team at Footnote Press. It's a joy and honour to be part of such an extraordinary roster of authors. Last but not least, a massive thank you to my editor Serena Arthur for her courage and care in helping birth this book.

Sunny Singh is a writer, novelist, public intellectual, and a champion for decolonisation and inclusion across all aspects of society.

She is the author of three critically acclaimed novels, *Hotel Arcadia*, *With Krishna's Eyes*, and *Nani's Book of Suicides*, a bestselling non-fiction book on lives of single women in India, a groundbreaking study of Amitabh Bachchan for the BFI's Film Star series, and the recent *A Bollywood State of Mind: A Journey into the World's Biggest Cinema*.

In 2017 she launched the celebrated Jhalak Prize for literature by writers of colour. She is also a founder of the Jhalak Foundation, which focuses on a range of literary, artistic and literacy initiatives in the UK and beyond.

Sunny lives in London where she is Professor of Creative Writing and Inclusion in the Arts at London Metropolitan University.